Praise for
# the Work of Iain M. Banks

"Banks is a phenomenon...writing pure science fiction of a peculiarly gnarly energy and elegance." —William Gibson

"Banks writes with a sophistication that will surprise anyone unfamiliar with modern science fiction." —*New York Times*

"Banks never lets up in a dizzying array of characters, mind-bending ideas, and dazzling action." —*Booklist*

"Few of us have been exposed to a talent so manifest and of such extraordinary breadth." —*New York Review of Science Fiction*

"Banks can summon up sense-of-wonder Big Concepts you've never seen before and display them with narration as deft as a conjuror's fingers." —syfy.com

"Nobody does it better." —*The Times*

# THE STATE OF THE ART

# IAIN M. BANKS

orbitbooks.net

Copyright © 1991 by Iain M. Banks

Illustrations copyright © 1991 by Nick Day

"Road of Skulls" first published in *20 under 35*, Sceptre 1988
"A Gift from the Culture" first published in *Interzone*, No. 20, 1987
"Odd Attachment" first published in *Arrows of Eros*, New English Library 1989
"Descendant" first published in "Tales from the Forbidden Planet," Titan Books 1987
"Cleaning Up" first published by the Birmingham Science Fiction Group on the occasion of Novacon 17, October 1987
"Piece" first published by the *Observer* magazine in 1989
"The State of the Art" first published in the United States in 1989 by Mark V. Ziesing
"Scratch" first published by *Fiction* magazine, volume 6 No. 6, in August 1987.

Cover design by Ben Prior & Nico Taylor | LBBG
Cover illustration by Julian Fischer
Author photograph by Ray Charles Redman

Orbit
Hachette Book Group
1290 Avenue of the Americas
New York, NY 10104
orbitbooks.net

First Orbit U.S. Edition: March 2024
Originally published in Great Britain by Orbit in 1991

Orbit is an imprint of Hachette Book Group.
The Orbit name and logo are registered trademarks of Little, Brown Book Group Limited.

The publisher is not responsible for websites (or their content) that are not owned by the publisher.

Orbit books may be purchased in bulk for business, educational, or promotional use. For information, please contact your local bookseller or the Hachette Book Group Special Markets Department at special.markets@hbgusa.com.

Library of Congress Control Number: 2023945886

ISBNs: 9780316565646 (trade paperback), 9780316565660 (ebook)

Printed in the United States of America

CW

10 9 8 7 6 5 4 3 2 1

*For John Jarrold*

# CONTENTS

# Road of Skulls

The ride's a little bumpy on the famous Road of Skulls...
"My *God*, what's happening!" Sammil Mc9 cried, waking up.

The cart he and his companion had hitched a ride on was shaking violently.

Mc9 put his grubby hands on the plank of rotten wood which formed one of the cart's sides and looked down at the legendary Road, wondering what had caused the cart's previously merely uncomfortable rattling to become a series of bone-jarring crashes. He expected to discover that they had lost a wheel, or that the snooze-prone carter had let the vehicle wander right off the Road into a boulderfield, but he saw neither of these things. He stared, goggle-eyed, at the Road surface for a moment, then collapsed back inside the cart.

"Golly," he said to himself, "I didn't know the Empire ever had enemies with heads *that* big. Retribution from beyond the grave, that's what this is." He looked forward; the cart's senile driver was still asleep, despite the vehicle's frenzied bouncing. Beyond him, the lop-eared old quadruped between the shafts was having some difficulty finding its footing on the oversized skulls forming that part of the Road, which led...Mc9 let his eyes follow the thin white line into the distance...to the City.

It lay on the horizon of the moor, a shimmering blur. Most of the fabled megalopolis was still below the horizon, but its sharp, glittering towers were unmistakable, even through the blue and shifting haze. Mc9 grinned as he saw it, then watched the silent, struggling horse-thing as it clopped and skidded its way along the Road; it was sweating heavily, and beset by a small cloud of flies buzzing around its ear-flapping head like bothersome electrons around some reluctant nucleus.

The old carter woke up and lashed inaccurately at the nag between the shafts, then nodded back into his slumber. Mc9 looked away and gazed out over the moor.

Usually the moor was a cold and desolate place, wrapped in wind and rain, but today it was blisteringly hot; the air reeked of marsh gases and the heath was sprinkled with tiny bright flowers. Mc9 sank back into the straw again, scratching and squirming as the cart bucked and heaved about him. He tried shifting the bundles of straw and the heaps of dried dung into more comfortable configurations, but failed. He was just thinking that the journey would seem very long, and be uncomfortable indeed if this outrageous juddering went on, when the crashes died away and the cart went back to its more normal rattling and squeaking. "Thank goodness *they* didn't hold out too long," Mc9 muttered to himself, and lay down again, closing his eyes.

...he was driving a haycart down a leafy lane. Birds were chirping, the wine was cool, money weighed in his pocket...

He wasn't quite asleep when his companion—whose name, despite their long association, Mc9 had never bothered to find out—surfaced from beneath the straw and dung beside him and said, "Retribution?"

"Eh? What?" Mc9 said, startled.

"What retribution?"

"Oh," Mc9 said, rubbing his face and grimacing as he squinted at the sun, high in the blue-green sky. "The retribution inflicted upon us as Subjects of the Reign, by the deceased Enemies of the Beloved Empire."

The small companion, whose spectacular grubbiness was only partially obscured by a covering of debatably less filthy straw, blinked furiously and shook his head. "No...me mean, what 'retribution' mean?"

"I just told you," Mc9 complained. "Getting back at somebody."

"Oh," said the companion, and sat mulling this over while Mc9 drifted off to sleep again.

...there were three young milkmaids walking ahead of his

haycart; he drew level and they accepted a ride. He reached down to...

His companion dug him in the ribs. "Like when me take too many bedclothes and you kick I out of bed, or me drink your wine and you make I drink three guts of laxative beer, or when you pregnanted that governor's daughter and him set the Strategic Debt Collectors on you, or someplace doesn't pay all its taxes and Its Majesty orders the first born of every family have their Birth Certificates endorsed, or...?"

Mc9, who was well used to his companion employing the verbal equivalent of a Reconnaissance By Fire, held up one hand to stem this flood of examples. His companion continued mumbling away despite the hand over his mouth. Finally the mumbling stopped.

"Yes," Mc9 told him. "That's right." He took his hand away.

"Or is it like when—?"

"Hey," Mc9 said brightly. "How about I tell you a story?"

"Oh, a *story*," beamed his companion, clutching at Mc9's sleeve in anticipation. "A story would be..." his grimy features contorted like a drying mudflat as he struggled to find a suitable adjective. "...Nice."

"OK. Let go my sleeve and pass me the wine to wet my throat."

"Oh," Mc9's companion said, and looked suddenly wary and doubtful. He glanced over the front of the cart, past the snoring driver and the toiling beast pulling them, and saw the City, still just a distant shimmer at the end of the Road's bleached ribbon of bone. "OK," he sighed.

He handed the wineskin to Mc9, who guzzled about half of what was left before the squealing, protesting companion succeeded in tearing it from his grasp, spilling most of the remainder over the two of them and squirting a jet of the liquid spattering over the neck of the snoring driver, and on out as far as the head of the horse-like animal (which lapped appreciatively at the drops spilling down its sweat-matted face).

The decrepit driver woke with a start and looked around wildly, rubbing his damp neck, waving his frayed whip and apparently fully expecting to have to repel robbers, cut-throats and villains.

Mc9 and his companion grinned sheepishly at him when he turned to look down at them. He scowled, dried his neck with a rag, then turned round and relapsed into his slumber.

"Thanks," Mc9 told his companion. He wiped his face and sucked at one of the fresh wine stains on his shirt.

The companion took a careful, dainty sip of wine, then twisted the stopper firmly back into the gut and placed it behind his neck as he lay back. Mc9 belched, yawned.

"Yes," his companion said earnestly. "Tell I a story. Me would love to hear a story. Tell I a story of love and hate and death and tragedy and comedy and horror and joy and sarcasm, tell I about great deeds and tiny deeds and valiant people and hill people and huge giants and dwarfs, tell I about brave women and beautiful men and great sorcerorcerors... and about unenchanted swords and strange, archaic powers and horrible, sort of ghastly...things that, uhm...shouldn't be living, and...ahm, funny diseases and general mishaps. Yeah, me like. Tell I. Me want."

Mc9 was falling asleep again, having had not the slightest intention of telling his companion a story in the first place. The companion prodded him in the back.

"Hey!" He prodded harder. "Hey! The story! No go to sleep! What about the story?"

"Fornicate the story," Mc9 said sleepily, not opening his eyes.

"WAA!" the companion said. The carter woke up, turned round and clipped him across the ear. The companion went quiet and sat there, rubbing the side of his head. He prodded Mc9 again and whispered, "You said you'd tell me a story!"

"Oh, read a book," mumbled Mc9, snuggling into the straw.

The small companion made a hissing noise and sat back, his lips tight and his little hands clenched under his armpits. He glared at the Road stretching back to the wavering horizon.

After a while, the companion shrugged, reached under the wineskin for his satchel and took out a small, fat black book.

He prodded Mc9 once more. "All we've got is this Bible," he told him. "What bit should me read?"

"Just open it at random," Mc9 mumbled from his sleep.

The companion opened the Bible at Random, Chapter Six, and read:

"Yeah yeah yeah, verily I say unto you: Forget not that there *are* two sides to every story: a right side *and* a wrong side."

The companion shook his head and threw the book over the side of the cart.

The road went ever on. The carter snuffled and snored, the sweating nag panted and struggled, while Mc9 smiled in his sleep and moaned a little. His companion passed the time by squeezing blackheads from his nose, and then replacing them.

...they had stopped at the ford through the shady brook, where the milkmaids were eventually persuaded to come for a swim, dressed only in their thin, clinging...

Actually, the horse-like beast pulling the cart was the famous poet-scribe Abrusci from the planet Wellitisn'tmarkedon*my-chartlieutenant*, and she could have told the bored companion any number of fascinating stories from the times before the Empire's Pacification and Liberation of her homeworld.

She could also have told them that the City was moving away from them across the moor as fast as they moved towards it, trundling across the endless heath on its millions of giant wheels as the continuous supply of vanquished Enemies of the Empire provided more trophies to be cemented into place on the famous Road of Skulls...

But that, like they say, is another story.

# A Gift from the Culture

**M**oney is a sign of poverty. This is an old Culture saying I remember every now and again, especially when I'm being tempted to do something I know I shouldn't, and there's money involved (when is there not?).

I looked at the gun, lying small and precise in Cruizell's broad, scarred hand, and the first thing I thought—after: Where the hell did they get one of *those?*—was: Money is a sign of poverty. However appropriate the thought might have been, it wasn't much help.

I was standing outside a no-credit gambling club in Vreccis Low City in the small hours of a wet weeknight, looking at a pretty, toy-like handgun while two large people I owed a lot of money to asked me to do something extremely dangerous and worse than illegal. I was weighing up the relative attractions of trying to run away (they'd shoot me), refusing (they'd beat me up; probably I'd spend the next few weeks developing a serious medical bill), and doing what Kaddus and Cruizell asked me to do, knowing that while there was a chance I'd get away with it—uninjured, and solvent again—the most likely outcome was a messy and probably slow death while assisting the security services with their enquiries.

Kaddus and Cruizell were offering me all my markers back, plus—once the thing was done—a tidy sum on top, just to show there were no hard feelings.

I suspected they didn't anticipate having to pay the final instalment of the deal.

So, I knew that logically what I ought to do was tell them where to shove their fancy designer pistol, and accept a theoretically painful but probably not terminal beating. Hell, I could switch the pain off (having a Culture background does have some advantages), but what about that hospital bill?

I was up to my scalp in debt already.

"What's the matter, Wrobik?" Cruizell drawled, taking a step nearer, under the shelter of the club's dripping eaves. Me with my back against the warm wall, the smell of wet pavements in my nose and a taste like metal in my mouth. Kaddus and Cruizell's limousine idled at the kerb; I could see the driver inside, watching us through an open window. Nobody passed on the street outside the narrow alley. A police cruiser flew over, high up, lights flashing through the rain and illuminating the underside of the rain clouds over the city. Kaddus looked up briefly, then ignored the passing craft. Cruizell shoved the gun towards me. I tried to shrink back.

"Take the gun, Wrobik," Kaddus said tiredly. I licked my lips, stared down at the pistol.

"I can't," I said. I stuck my hands in my coat pockets.

"Sure you can," Cruizell said. Kaddus shook his head.

"Wrobik, don't make things difficult for yourself; take the gun. Just touch it first, see if our information is correct. Go on; take it." I stared, transfixed, at the small pistol. "Take the gun, Wrobik. Just remember to point it at the ground, not at us; the driver's got a laser on you and he might think you meant to use the gun on us...come on; take it, touch it."

I couldn't move, I couldn't think. I just stood, hypnotized. Kaddus took hold of my right wrist and pulled my hand from my pocket. Cruizell held the gun up near my nose; Kaddus forced my hand onto the pistol. My hand closed round the grip like something lifeless.

The gun came to life; a couple of lights blinked dully, and the small screen above the grip glowed, flickering round the edges. Cruizell dropped his hand, leaving me holding the pistol; Kaddus smiled thinly.

"There, that wasn't difficult, now was it?" Kaddus said. I held the gun and tried to imagine using it on the two men, but I knew I couldn't, whether the driver had me covered or not.

"Kaddus," I said, "I can't do this. Something else; I'll do anything else, but I'm not a hit-man; I can't—"

"You don't have to be an expert, Wrobik," Kaddus said quietly. "All you have to be is...whatever the hell you are. After that, you just point and squirt: like you do with your boyfriend." He grinned and winked at Cruizell, who bared some teeth. I shook my head.

"This is crazy, Kaddus. Just because the thing switches on for me—"

"Yeah; isn't that funny." Kaddus turned to Cruizell, looking up to the taller man's face and smiling. "Isn't that funny, Wrobik here being an alien? And him looking just like us."

"An alien *and* queer," Cruizell rumbled, scowling. "Shit."

"Look," I said, staring at the pistol, "it...this thing, it...it might not work," I finished lamely. Kaddus smiled.

"It'll work. A ship's a big target. You won't miss." He smiled again.

"But I thought they had protection against—"

"Lasers and kinetics they can deal with, Wrobik; this is something different. I don't know the technical details; I just know our radical friends paid a lot of money for this thing. That's enough for me."

Our radical friends. This was funny, coming from Kaddus. Probably he meant the Bright Path. People he'd always considered bad for business, just terrorists. I'd have imagined he'd sell them to the police on general principles, even if they did offer him lots of money. Was he starting to hedge his bets, or just being greedy? They have a saying here: Crime whispers; money talks.

"But there'll be people on the ship, not just—"

"You won't be able to see them. Anyway; they'll be some of the Guard, Naval brass, some Administration flunkeys, Secret Service agents...What do you care about them?" Kaddus patted my damp shoulder. "You can do it."

I looked away from his tired grey eyes, down at the gun, quiet in my fist, small screen glowing faintly. Betrayed by my own skin, my own touch. I thought about that hospital bill again. I felt like crying, but that wasn't the done thing amongst the men here, and what could I say? *I was a woman. I was Culture.* But I had renounced these things, and now I am a man, and now I am here in the Free City of Vreccis, where nothing is free.

"All right," I said, a bitterness of my mouth, "I'll do it."

Cruizell looked disappointed. Kaddus nodded. "Good. The ship arrives Ninthday; you know what it looks like?" I nodded. "So you won't have any problems," Kaddus smiled thinly. "You'll be able to see it from almost anywhere in the City." He pulled out some cash and stuffed it into my coat pocket. "Get yourself a taxi. The underground's risky these days." He patted me lightly on the cheek; his hand smelt of expensive scents. "Hey, Wrobik; cheer up, yeah? You're going to shoot down a fucking starship. It'll be an experience." Kaddus laughed, looking at me and then at Cruizell, who laughed too, dutifully.

They went back to the car; it hummed into the night, tyres ripping at the rain-filled streets. I was left to watch the puddles grow, the gun hanging in my hand like guilt.

"I am a Light Plasma Projector, model LPP 91, series two, constructed in A/4882.4 at Manufactury Six in the Spanshacht-Trouferre Orbital, Ørvolöus Cluster. Serial number 3685706. Brain value point one. AM battery powered, rating: indefinite. Maximum power on single-bolt: $3.1 \times 8^{10}$ joules, recycle time 14 seconds. Maximum rate of fire: 260 RPS. Use limited to Culture genofixed individuals only through epidermal gene analysis. To use with gloves or light armour, access 'modes' store via command buttons. Unauthorized use is both prohibited and punishable. Skill requirement 12–75%C. Full instructions follow; use command buttons and screen to replay, search, pause or stop...

"Instructions, part one: Introduction. The LPP 91 is an

operationally intricate general-purpose 'peace'-rated weapon
not suitable for full battle use; its design and performance
parameters are based on the recommendations of—"

The gun sat on the table, telling me all about itself in a high,
tinny voice while I lay slumped in a lounger, staring out over
a busy street in Vreccis Low City. Underground freight trains
shook the rickety apartment block every few minutes, traffic
buzzed at street level, rich people and police moved through
the skies in fliers and cruisers, and above them all the starships sailed.

I felt trapped between these strata of purposeful movements.

Far in the distance over the city, I could just see the slender,
shining tower of the city's Lev tube, rising straight towards
and through the clouds, on its way to space. Why couldn't
the Admiral use the Lev instead of making a big show of
returning from the stars in his own ship? Maybe he thought
a glorified elevator was too undignified. Vainglorious bastards,
all of them. They deserved to die (if you wanted to take that
attitude), but why did I have to be the one to kill them? Goddamned phallic starships.

Not that the Lev was any less prick-like, and anyway, no
doubt if the Admiral had been coming down by the tube Kaddus and Cruizell would have told me to shoot *it* down; holy
shit. I shook my head.

I was holding a long glass of jahl—Vreccis City's cheapest
strong booze. It was my second glass, but I wasn't enjoying
it. The gun chattered on, speaking to the sparsely furnished
main room of our apartment. I was waiting for Maust, missing him even more than usual. I looked at the terminal on
my wrist; according to the time display he should be back
any moment now. I looked out into the weak, watery light of
dawn. I hadn't slept yet.

The gun talked on. It used Marain, of course; the Culture's language. I hadn't heard that spoken for nearly eight
standard years, and hearing it now I felt sad and foolish. My
birthright; my people, my language. Eight years away, eight

years in the wilderness. My great adventure, my renunciation of what seemed to me sterile and lifeless to plunge into a more vital society, my grand gesture...well, now it seemed like an empty gesture, now it looked like a stupid, petulant thing to have done.

I drank some more of the sharp-tasting spirit. The gun gibbered on, talking about beam-spread diameters, gyroscopic weave patterns, gravity-contour mode, line-of-sight mode, curve shots, spatter and pierce settings...I thought about glanding something soothing and cool, but I didn't; I had vowed not to use those cunningly altered glands eight years ago, and I'd broken that vow only twice, both times when I was in severe pain. Had I been courageous I'd have had the whole damn lot taken out, returned to their human-normal state, our original animal inheritance...but I am not courageous. I dread pain, and cannot face it naked, as these people do. I admire them, fear them, still cannot understand them. Not even Maust. In fact, least of all Maust. Perhaps you cannot ever love what you completely understand.

Eight years in exile, lost to the Culture; never hearing that silky, subtle, complexly simple language, and now when I do hear Marain, it's from a gun, telling me how to fire it so I can kill...what? Hundreds of people? Maybe thousands; it will depend on where the ship falls, whether it explodes (could primitive starships explode? I had no idea; that was never my field). I took another drink, shook my head. I couldn't do it.

I am Wrobik Sennkil, Vreccile citizen number...(I always forget; it's on my papers), male, prime race, aged thirty; part-time freelance journalist (between jobs at the moment), and full-time gambler (I tend to lose but I enjoy myself, or at least I did until last night). But I am, also, still Bahlln-Euchersa Wrobich Vress Schennil dam Flaysse, citizen of the Culture, born female, species mix too complicated to remember, aged sixty-eight, standard, and one-time member of the Contact section.

And a renegade; I chose to exercise the freedom the Culture is so proud of bestowing upon its inhabitants by leaving it altogether. It let me go, even helped me, reluctant though I was (but could I have forged my own papers, made all the arrangements by myself? No, but at least, after my education into the ways of the Vreccile Economic Community, and after the module rose, dark and silent, back into the night sky and the waiting ship, I have turned only twice to the Culture's legacy of altered biology, and not once to its artefacts. Until now; the gun rambles on). I abandoned a paradise I considered dull for a cruel and greedy system bubbling with life and incident; a place I thought I might find...what? I don't know. I didn't know when I left and I don't know yet, though at least here I found Maust, and when I am with him my searching no longer seems so lonely.

Until last night that search still seemed worthwhile. Now utopia sends a tiny package of destruction, a casual, accidental message.

Where *did* Kaddus and Cruizell get the thing? The Culture guards its weaponry jealously, even embarrassedly. You can't buy Culture weapons, at least not from the Culture. I suppose things go missing though; there is so much of everything in the Culture that objects must be mislaid occasionally. I took another drink, listening to the gun, and watching that watery, rainy-season sky over the rooftops, towers, aerials, dishes and domes of the Great City. Maybe guns slip out of the Culture's manicured grasp more often than other products do; they betoken danger, they signify threat, and they will only be needed where there must be a fair chance of losing them, so they must disappear now and again, be taken as prizes.

That, of course, is why they're built with inhibiting circuits which only let the weapons work for Culture people (sensible, non-violent, non-acquisitive Culture people, who *of course* would only use a gun in self-defence, for example, if threatened by some comparative barbarian...oh the self-satisfied Culture: its imperialism of smugness). And even this gun is antique; not obsolescent (for that is not a concept the Culture really approves of—it builds to last), but outdated; hardly more intelligent than a household pet, whereas modern Culture weaponry is sentient.

The Culture probably doesn't even make handguns any more. I've seen what it calls Personal Armed Escort Drones, and if, somehow, one of those fell into the hands of people like Kaddus and Cruizell, it would immediately signal for help, use its motive power to try and escape, shoot to injure or even kill anybody trying to use or trap it, attempt to bargain its way out, and destruct if it thought it was going to be taken apart or otherwise interfered with.

I drank some more jahl. I looked at the time again; Maust was late. The club always closed promptly, because of the police. They weren't allowed to talk to the customers after work: he always came straight back...I felt the start of fear, but pushed it away. Of course he'd be all right. I had other things to think about. I had to think this thing through. More jahl.

No, I couldn't do it. I left the Culture because it bored me, but also because the evangelical, interventionist morality of Contact sometimes meant doing just the sort of thing we were supposed to prevent others doing; starting wars, assassinating...all of it, all the bad things...I was never involved with Special Circumstances directly, but I knew what went on (Special Circumstances; Dirty Tricks, in other words. The Culture's tellingly unique euphemism). I refused to live with such hypocrisy and chose instead this honestly selfish and avaricious society, which doesn't pretend to be good, just ambitious.

But I have lived here as I lived there, trying not to hurt others, trying just to be myself; and I cannot be myself by destroying a ship full of people, even if they are some of the rulers of this cruel and callous society. I can't use the gun; I can't let Kaddus and Cruizell find me. And I will not go back, head bowed, to the Culture.

I finished the glass of jahl.

I had to get out. There were other cities, other planets,

besides Vreccis; I'd just had to run; run and hide. Would Maust come with me though? I looked at the time again; he was half an hour late. Not like him. Why was he late? I went to the window, looking down to the street, searching for him.

A police APC rumbled through the traffic. Just a routine cruise; siren off, guns stowed. It was heading for the Outworlder's Quarter, where the police had been making shows of strength recently. No sign of Maust's svelte shape swinging through the crowds.

Always the worry. That he might be run over, that the police might arrest him at the club (indecency, corrupting public morals, and homosexuality; that great crime, even worse than not making your pay-off!), and, of course, the worry that he might meet somebody else.

Maust. Come home safely, come home to me.

I remember feeling cheated when I discovered, towards the end of my regendering, that I still felt drawn to men. That was long ago, when I was happy in the Culture, and like many people I had wondered what it would be like to love those of my own original sex; it seemed terribly unfair that my desires did not alter with my physiology. It took Maust to make me feel I had not been cheated. Maust made everything better. Maust was my breath of life.

Anyway, I would not be a woman in this society.

I decided I needed a refill. I walked past the table.

"...will not affect the line-stability of the weapon, though recoil will be increased on power-priority, or power decreased—"

"Shut up!" I shouted at the gun, and made a clumsy attempt to hit its Off button; my hand hit the pistol's stubby barrel. The gun skidded across the table and fell to the floor.

"Warning!" The gun shouted. "There are no user-serviceable parts inside! Irreversible deactivation will result if any attempt is made to dismantle or—"

"Quiet, you little bastard," I said (and it did go quiet). I picked it up and put it in the pocket of a jacket hanging over a chair. Damn the Culture; damn all guns. I went to get more drink, a heaviness inside me as I looked at the time again. Come home, please come home...and then come away, come away with me...

I fell asleep in front of the screen, a knot of dull panic in my belly competing with the spinning sensation in my head as I watched the news and worried about Maust, trying not to think of too many things. The news was full of executed terrorists and famous victories in small, distant wars against aliens, out-worlders, subhumans. The last report I remember was about a riot in a city on another planet; there was no mention of civilian deaths, but I remember a shot of a broad street littered with crumpled shoes. The item closed with an injured policeman being interviewed in hospital.

I had my recurring nightmare, reliving the demonstration I was caught up in three years ago; looking, horrified, at a wall of drifting, sun-struck stun gas and seeing a line of police mounts come charging out of it, somehow more appalling than armoured cars or even tanks, not because of the visored riders with their long shock-batons, but because the tall animals were also armoured and gas-masked; monsters from a ready-made, mass-produced dream; terrorizing.

Maust found me there hours later, when he got back. The club had been raided and he hadn't been allowed to contact me. He held me as I cried, shushing me back to sleep.

"Wrobik, I can't. Risåret's putting on a new show next season and he's looking for new faces; it'll be big-time, straight stuff. A High City deal. I can't leave now; I've got my foot in the door. Please understand." He reached over the table to take my hand. I pulled it away.

"I can't do what they're asking me to do. I can't stay. So I have to go; there's nothing else I can do." My voice was dull. Maust started to clear away the plates and containers, shaking his long, graceful head. I hadn't eaten much; partly hangover, partly nerves. It was a muggy, enervating mid-morning; the tenement's conditioning plant had broken down again.

"Is what they're asking really so terrible?" Maust pulled his robe tighter, balancing plates expertly. I watched his slim back as he moved to the kitchen. "I mean, you won't even tell me. Don't you trust me?" His voice echoed.

What could I say? That I didn't know if I did trust him? That I loved him but: only he had known I was an outworlder. That had been my secret, and I'd told only him. So how did Kaddus and Cruizell know? How did Bright Path know? My sinuous, erotic, faithless dancer. Did you think because I always remained silent that I didn't know of all the times you deceived me?

"Maust, please; it's better that you don't know."

"Oh," Maust laughed distantly; that aching, beautiful sound, tearing at me. "How terribly dramatic. You're protecting me. How awfully gallant."

"Maust, this is serious. These people want me to do something I just can't do. If I don't do it they'll... they'll at least hurt me, badly. I don't know what they'll do. They... they might even try to hurt me through you. That was why I was so worried when you were late; I thought maybe they'd taken you."

"My dear, poor Wrobbie," Maust said, looking out from the kitchen, "it has been a long day; I think I pulled a muscle during my last number, we may not get paid after the raid—Stelmer's sure to use that as an excuse even if the filth didn't swipe the takings—and my ass is still sore from having one of those queer-bashing pigs poking his finger around inside me. Not as romantic as your dealings with gangsters and baddies, but important to me. I've enough to worry about. You're overreacting. Take a pill or something; go back to sleep; it'll look better later." He winked at me, disappeared. I listened to him moving about in the kitchen. A police siren moaned overhead. Music filtered through from the apartment below.

I went to the door of the kitchen. Maust was drying his hands. "They want me to shoot down the starship bringing the Admiral of the Fleet back on Ninthday," I told him. Maust looked blank for a second, then sniggered. He came up to me, held me by the shoulders.

"Really? And then what? Climb the outside of the Lev and fly to the sun on your magic bicycle?" He smiled tolerantly, amused. I put my hands on his and removed them slowly from my shoulders.

"No. I just have to shoot down the ship, that's all. I have… they gave me a gun that can do it." I took the gun from the jacket. He frowned, shaking his head, looked puzzled for a second, then laughed again.

"With that, my love? I doubt you could stop a motorized pogo-stick with that little—"

"Maust, please; believe me. This can do it. My people made it and the ship…the state has no defence against something like this."

Maust snorted, then took the gun from me. Its lights flicked off. "How do you switch it on?" He turned it over in his hand.

"By touching it; but only I can do it. It reads the genetic make-up of my skin, knows I am Culture. Don't look at me like that; it's true. Look." I showed him. I had the gun recite the first part of its monologue and switched the tiny screen to holo. Maust inspected the gun while I held it.

"You know," he said after a while, "this might be rather valuable."

"No, it's worthless to anyone else. It'll only work for me, and you can't get round its fidelities; it'll deactivate."

"How…faithful," Maust said, sitting down and looking steadily at me. "How neatly everything must be arranged in your 'Culture.' I didn't really believe you when you told me that tale, did you know that, my love? I thought you were just trying to impress me. Now I think I believe you."

I crouched down in front of him, put the gun on the table and my hands on his lap. "Then believe me that I can't do what they're asking, and that I am in danger; perhaps we both are. We have to leave. Now. Today or tomorrow. Before they think of another way to make me do this."

Maust smiled, ruffled my hair. "So fearful, eh? So desperately anxious." He bent, kissed my forehead. "Wrobbie, Wrobbie; I can't come with you. Go if you feel you must, but I can't come with you. Don't you know what this chance means to me? All my life I've wanted this; I may not get another opportunity. I have to stay, whatever. You go; go for as long as you must and don't tell me where you've gone. That way they can't use me, can they? Get in touch through a friend, once the dust has settled. Then we'll see. Perhaps you can come back; perhaps I'll have missed my big chance anyway and I'll come to join you. It'll be all right. We'll work something out."

I let my head fall to his lap, wanting to cry. "I can't leave you."

He hugged me, rocking me. "Oh, you'll probably find you're glad of the change. You'll be a hit wherever you go, my beauty; I'll probably have to kill some knife-fighter to win you back."

"Please, please come with me," I sobbed into his gown.

"I can't, my love, I just can't. I'll come to wave you goodbye, but I can't come with you."

He held me while I cried; the gun lay silent and dull on the table at his side, surrounded by the debris of our meal.

I was leaving. Fire escape from the flat just before dawn, over two walls clutching my travelling bag, a taxi from General Thetropsis Avenue to Intercontinental Station…then I'd catch a Railtube train to Bryme and take the Lev there, hoping for a standby on almost anything heading Out, either trans or inter. Maust had lent me some of his savings, and I still had a little high-rate credit left; I could make it. I left my terminal in the apartment. It would have been useful, but the rumours are true; the police can trace them, and I wouldn't put it past Kaddus and Cruizell to have a tame cop in the relevant department.

The station was crowded. I felt fairly safe in the high, echoing halls, surrounded by people and business. Maust was coming from the club to see me off; he'd promised to make sure he wasn't followed. I had just enough time to leave the gun at Left Luggage. I'd post the key to Kaddus, try to leave him a little less murderous.

There was a long queue at Left Luggage; I stood, exasperated, behind some naval cadets. They told me the delay was caused by the porters searching all bags and cases for bombs; a new security measure. I left the queue to go and meet Maust; I'd have to get rid of the gun somewhere else. Post the damn thing, or even just drop it in a waste bin.

I waited in the bar, sipping at something innocuous. I kept looking at my wrist, then feeling foolish. The terminal was back at the apartment; use a public phone, look for a clock. Maust was late.

There was a screen in the bar, showing a news bulletin. I shook off the absurd feeling that somehow I was already a wanted man, face liable to appear on the news broadcast, and watched today's lies to take my mind off the time.

They mentioned the return of the Admiral of the Fleet, due in two days. I looked at the screen, smiling nervously. *Yeah, and you'll never know how close the bastard came to getting blown out of the skies.* For a moment or two I felt important, almost heroic.

Then the bombshell; just a mention—an aside, tacked on, the sort of thing they'd have cut had the programme been a few seconds over—that the Admiral would be bringing a guest with him; an ambassador from the Culture. I choked on my drink.

Was *that* who I'd really have been aiming at if I'd gone ahead?

What was the Culture doing anyway? An ambassador? The Culture knew everything about the Vreccile Economic Community, and was watching, analyzing; content to leave ill enough alone for now. The Vreccile people had little idea how advanced or widely spread the Culture was, though the court and Navy had a fairly good idea. Enough to make them slightly (though had they known it, still not remotely sufficiently) paranoid. What was an ambassador for?

And who was really behind the attempt on the ship? Bright Path would be indifferent to the fate of a single outworlder compared to the propaganda coup of pulling down a starship, but what if the gun hadn't come from them, but from a grouping in the court itself, or from the Navy? The VEC had problems; social problems, political problems. Maybe the President and his cronies were thinking about asking the Culture for aid. The price might involve the sort of changes some of the more corrupt officials would find terminally threatening to their luxurious lifestyles.

Shit, I didn't know; maybe the whole attempt to take out the ship was some loony in Security or the Navy trying to settle an old score, or just skip the next few rungs on the promotion ladder. I was still thinking about this when they paged me.

I sat still. The station PA called for me, three times. A phonecall. I told myself it was just Maust, calling to say he had been delayed; he knew I was leaving the terminal at the apartment so he couldn't call me direct. But would he announce my name all over a crowded station when he knew I was trying to leave quietly and unseen? Did he still take it all so lightly? I didn't want to answer that call. I didn't even want to think about it.

My train was leaving in ten minutes; I picked up my bag. The PA asked for me again, this time mentioning Maust's name. So I had no choice.

I went to Information. It was a viewcall.

"Wrobik," Kaddus sighed, shaking his head. He was in some office; anonymous, bland. Maust was standing, pale and frightened, just behind Kaddus' seat. Cruizell stood right behind Maust, grinning over his slim shoulder. Cruizell moved slightly, and Maust flinched. I saw him bite his lip. "Wrobik," Kaddus said again. "Were you going to leave so soon? I thought we had a date, yes?"

"Yes," I said quietly, looking at Maust's eyes. "Silly of me. I'll...stick around for...a couple of days. Maust, I—" The screen went grey.

I turned round slowly in the booth and looked at my bag, where the gun was. I picked the bag up. I hadn't realized how heavy it was.

I stood in the park, surrounded by dripping trees and worn rocks. Paths carved into the tired top-soil led in various directions. The earth smelled warm and damp. I looked down from the top of the gently sloped escarpment to where pleasure boats sailed in the dusk, lights reflecting on the still waters of the boating lake. The duskward quarter of the city was a hazy platform of light in the distance. I heard birds calling from the trees around me.

The aircraft lights of the Lev rose like a rope of flashing red beads into the blue evening sky; the port at the Lev's summit shone, still uneclipsed, in sunlight a hundred kilometres overhead. Lasers, ordinary searchlights and chemical fireworks began to make the sky bright above the Parliament buildings and the Great Square of the Inner City; a display to greet the returning, victorious Admiral, and maybe the ambassador from the Culture, too. I couldn't see the ship yet.

I sat down on a tree stump, drawing my coat about me. The gun was in my hand; on, ready, ranged, set. I had tried to be thorough and professional, as though I knew what I was doing; I'd even left a hired motorbike in some bushes on the far side of the escarpment, down near the busy parkway. I might actually get away with this. So I told myself, anyway. I looked at the gun.

I considered using it to try and rescue Maust, or maybe using it to kill myself; I'd even considered taking it to the police (another, slower form of suicide). I'd also considered calling Kaddus and telling him I'd lost it, it wasn't working, I couldn't kill a fellow Culture citizen...anything. But in the end; nothing.

If I wanted Maust back I had to do what I'd agreed to do.

Something glinted in the skies above the city; a pattern of falling, golden lights. The central light was brighter and larger than the others.

I had thought I could feel no more, but there was a sharp taste in my mouth, and my hands were shaking. Perhaps I would go berserk, once the ship was down, and attack the Lev too; bring the whole thing smashing down (or would part of it go spinning off into space? Maybe I ought to do it just to see). I could bombard half the city from here (hell, don't forget the curve shots; I could bombard the *whole* damn city from here); I could bring down the escort vessels and attacking planes and police cruisers; I could give the Vreccile the biggest shock they've ever had, before they got me…

The ships were over the city. Out of the sunlight, their laser-proof mirror hulls were duller now. They were still falling; maybe five kilometres up. I checked the gun again.

Maybe it wouldn't work, I thought.

Lasers shone in the dust and grime above the city, producing tight spots on high and wispy clouds. Searchlight beams faded and spread in the same haze, while fireworks burst and slowly fell, twinkling and sparkling. The sleek ships dropped majestically to meet the welcoming lights. I looked about the tree-lined ridge; alone. A warm breeze brought the grumbling sound of the parkway traffic to me.

I raised the gun and sighted. The formation of ships appeared on the holo display, the scene noon-bright. I adjusted the magnification, fingered a command stud; the gun locked onto the flagship, became rock-steady in my hand. A flashing white point in the display marked the centre of the vessel.

I looked round again, my heart hammering, my hand held by the field-anchored gun. Still nobody came to stop me. My eyes stung. The ships hung a few hundred metres above the state buildings of the Inner City. The outer vessels remained there; the centre craft, the flagship, stately and massive, a mirror held up to the glittering city, descended towards the Great Square. The gun dipped in my hand, tracking it.

Maybe the Culture ambassador wasn't aboard the damn ship anyway. This whole thing might be a Special Circumstances set-up; perhaps the Culture was ready to interfere now and it amused the planning Minds to have me, a heretic, push things over the edge. The Culture ambassador might have been a ruse, just in case I started to suspect...I didn't know. I didn't know anything. I was floating on a sea of possibilities, but parched of choices.

I squeezed the trigger.

The gun leapt backwards, light flared all around me. A blinding line of brilliance flicked, seemingly instantaneously, from me to the starship ten kilometres away. There was a sharp detonation of sound somewhere inside my head. I was thrown off the tree stump.

When I sat up again the ship had fallen. The Great Square blazed with flames and smoke and strange, bristling tongues of some terrible lightning; the remaining lasers and fireworks were made dull. I stood, shaking, ears ringing, and stared at what I'd done. Late-reacting sprinterceptiles from the escorts criss-crossed the air above the wreck and slammed into the ground, automatics fooled by the sheer velocity of the plasma bolt. Their warheads burst brightly among the boulevards and buildings of the Inner City, a bruise upon a bruise.

The noise of the first explosion smacked and rumbled over the park.

The police and the escort ships themselves were starting to react. I saw the lights of police cruisers rise strobing from the Inner City; the escort craft began to turn slowly above the fierce, flickering radiations of the wreck.

I pocketed the gun and ran down the damp path towards the bike, away from the escarpment's lip. Behind my eyes, burnt there, I could still see the line of light that had briefly joined me to the starship; bright path indeed, I thought, and nearly laughed. A bright path in the soft darkness of the mind.

I raced down to join all the other poor folk on the run.

# Odd Attachment

D epressed and dejected, his unrequited love like a stony weight inside him, Fropome looked longingly at the sky, then shook his head slowly and stared disconsolately down at the meadow in front of him.

A nearby grazer cub, eating its way across the grassy plain with the rest of the herd, started cuffing one of its siblings. Normally their master would have watched the pretended fight with some amusement, but today he responded with a low creaking noise which ought to have warned the hot-blooded little animals. One of the tumbling cubs looked up briefly at Fropome, but then resumed the tussle. Fropome flicked out a vine-limb, slapping the two cubs across their rumps. They squealed, untangled, and stumbled mewling and yelping to their mothers on the outskirts of the herd.

Fropome watched them go, then—with a rustling noise very like a sigh—returned to looking at the bright orange sky. He forgot about the grazers and the prairie and thought again about his love.

His lady-love, his darling, the One for whom he would gladly climb any hillock, wade any lakelet; all that sort of thing. His love; his cruel, cold, heartless, uncaring love.

He felt crushed, dried-up inside whenever he thought of her. She seemed so unfeeling, so unconcerned. How could she be so dismissive? Even if she didn't love him in return, you'd have thought at least she'd be flattered to have somebody express their undying love for her. Was he so unattractive? Did she actually feel insulted that he worshipped her? If she did, why did she ignore him? If his attentions were unwelcome, why didn't she say so?

But she said nothing. She acted as though all he'd said,

everything he'd tried to express to her was just some embarrassing slip, a gaffe best ignored.

He didn't understand it. Did she think he would say such things lightly? Did she imagine he hadn't worried over what to say and how to say it, and where and when? He'd stopped eating! He hadn't slept for nights! He was starting to turn brown and curl up at the edges! Food-birds were setting up roosts in his nestraps!

A grazer cub nuzzled his side. He picked the furry little animal up in a vine, lifted it up to his head, stared at it with his four front eyes, sprayed it with irritant and flung it whimpering into a nearby bush.

The bush shook itself and made a grumbling noise. Fropome apologized to it as the grazer cub disentangled itself and scuttled off, scratching furiously.

Fropome would rather have been alone with his melancholy, but he had to watch over the grazer herd, keeping them out of acidcloys, pitplants and digastids, sheltering them from the foodbirds' stupespittle and keeping them away from the ponderously poised boulderbeasts.

Everything was so predatory. Couldn't love be different? Fropome shook his withered foliage.

Surely she must feel *something*. They'd been friends for seasons now; they got on well together, they found the same things amusing, they held similar opinions...if they were so alike in these respects, how could he feel such desperate, feverish passion for her and she feel nothing for him? Could this most basic root of the soul be so different when everything else seemed so in accord?

She *must* feel something for him. It was absurd to think she could feel nothing. She just didn't want to appear too forward. Her reticence was only caution; understandable, even commendable. She didn't want to commit herself too quickly... that was all. She was innocent as an unopened bud, shy as a moonbloom, modest as a leaf-wrapped heart...

...and pure as a star in the sky, Fropome thought. As pure,

and as remote. He gazed at a bright, new star in the sky, trying to convince himself she might return his love.

The star moved.

Fropome watched it.

The star twinkled, moved slowly across the sky, gradually brightening. Fropome made a wish on it: *Be an omen, be the sign that she loves me!* Perhaps it was a lucky star. He'd never been superstitious before, but love had strange effects on the vegetable heart.

If only he could be sure of her, he thought, gazing at the slowly falling star. He wasn't impatient; he would gladly wait for ever if he only knew she cared. It was the uncertainty that tormented him and left his hopes and fears toing-and-froing in such an agonizing way.

He looked almost affectionately at the grazers as they plodded their way around him, looking for a nice patch of uneaten grass or a yukscrub to defecate into.

Poor, simple creatures. And yet lucky, in a way; their life revolved around eating and sleeping, with no room in their low-browed little heads for anguish, no space in their furry chests for a ruptured capillary system.

Ah, what it must be, to have a simple, muscle heart!

He looked back to the sky. The evening stars seemed cool and calm, like dispassionate eyes, watching him. All except the falling star he'd wished on earlier.

He reflected briefly on the wisdom of wishing on such a transitory thing as a falling star...even one falling as slowly as this one seemed to be.

Oh, such disturbing, bud-like emotions! Such sapling gullibility and nervousness! Such cuttingish confusion and uncertainty!

The star still fell. It became brighter and brighter in the evening sky, lowering slowly and changing colour too; from sunwhite to moon-yellow to sky-orange to sunset-red. Fropome could hear its noise now; a dull roaring, like a strong wind disturbing short-tempered tree tops. The falling red star was no longer a single point of light; it had taken on a shape now, like a big seed pod.

It occurred to Fropome that this might indeed be a sign. Whatever it was had come from the stars, after all, and weren't stars the seeds of the Ancestors, shot so high they left the Earth and rooted in the celestial spheres of cold fire, all-seeing and all-knowing? Maybe the old stories were true after all, and the gods had come to tell him something momentous. A thrill of excitement rose within him. His limbs shook and his leaves beaded with moisture.

The pod was close now. It dipped and seemed to hesitate in the dark-orange sky. The pod's colour continued to deepen all the time, and Fropome realized it was *hot*; he could feel its warmth even from half a dozen reaches away.

It was an ellipsoid, a little smaller than he was. It flexed glittering roots from its bottom end, and glided through the air to land on the meadow with a sort of tentative deliberation, a couple of reaches away.

Fropome watched, thoroughly entranced. He didn't dare move. This might be important. A sign.

Everything was still; him, the grumbling bushes, the whispering grass, even the grazers looked puzzled.

The pod moved. Part of its casing fell back inside itself, producing a hole in the smooth exterior.

And something came out.

It was small and silver, and it walked on what might have been hind legs, or a pair of over-developed roots. It crossed to one of the grazers and started making noises at it. The grazer was so surprised it fell over. It lay staring up at the strange silver creature, blinking. Cubs ran, terrified, for their mothers. Other grazers looked at each other, or at Fropome, who still wasn't sure what to do.

The silver seedlet moved to another grazer and made noises at it. Confused, the grazer broke wind. The seedlet went to the animal's rear end and started speaking loudly there.

Fropome clapped a couple of vines together to request

respectfully the silver creature's attention, and made to spread the same two leaf-palms on the ground before the seedlet, in a gesture of supplication.

The creature leapt back, detached a bit of its middle with one of its stubby upper limbs, and pointed it at Fropome's vines. There was a flash of light and Fropome felt pain as his leaf-palms crisped and smoked. Instinctively, he lashed out at the creature, knocking it to the ground. The detached bit flew away across the meadow and hit a grazer cub on the flank.

Fropome was shocked, then angry. He held the struggling creature down with one undamaged vine while he inspected his injuries. The leaves would probably fall off and take days to re-grow. He used another limb to grasp the silver seedlet and bring it up to his eye cluster. He shook it, then up-ended it and stuck its top down at the leaves it had burned, and shook it again.

He brought it back up to inspect it more closely.

Damn funny thing to have come out of a seed pod, he thought, twisting the object this way and that. It looked a little like a grazer except it was thinner and silvery and the head was just a smooth reflective sphere. Fropome could not work out how it stayed upright. The over-large top made it look especially unbalanced. Possibly it wasn't meant to totter around for long; those pointed leg-like parts were probably roots. The thing wriggled in his grasp.

He tore off a little of the silvery outer bark and tasted it in a nestrap. He spat it out again. Not animal or vegetable; more like mineral. Very odd.

Root-pink tendrils squirmed at the end of the stubby upper limb, where Fropome had torn the outer covering off. Fropome looked at them, and wondered.

He took hold of one of the little pink filaments and pulled.

It came off with a faint "pop." Another, muffled-sounding noise came from the silvery top of the creature.

She loves me…

Fropome pulled off another tendril. Pop. Sap the colour of the setting sun dribbled out.

She loves me not...

Pop pop pop. He completed that set of tendrils.

She loves me...

Excited, Fropome pulled the covering off the end of the other upper limb. More tendrils.

...She loves me not.

A grazer cub came up and pulled at one of Fropome's lower branches. In its mouth it held the silvery creature's burner device, which had hit it on the flank. Fropome ignored it.

She loves me...

The grazer cub gave up pulling at Fropome's branch. It squatted down on the meadow, dropping the burner on the grass and prodding inquisitively at it with one paw.

The silvery seedlet was wriggling enthusiastically in Fropome's grip, thin red sap spraying everywhere.

Fropome completed the tendrils on the second upper limb.

Pop. She loves me not.

Oh no!

The grazer cub licked the burner, tapped it with its paw. One of the other cubs saw it playing with the bright toy and started ambling over towards it.

On a hunch, Fropome tore the covering off the blunt roots at the base of the creature. Ah ha!

She loves me...

The grazer cub at Fropome's side got bored with the shiny bauble; it was about to abandon the thing where it lay when it saw its sibling approaching, looking inquisitive. The first cub growled and started trying to pick the burner up with its mouth.

Pop...She loves me not!

Ah! Death! Shall my pollen never dust her perfectly formed ovaries? Oh, wicked, balanced, so blandly symmetrical *even* universe!

In his rage, Fropome ripped the silvery covering right off the lower half of the leaking, weakly struggling seedlet.

Oh unfair life! Oh treacherous stars!

The growling grazer cub hefted the burner device into its mouth.

Something clicked. The cub's head exploded.

Fropome didn't pay too much attention. He was staring intently at the bark-stripped creature he held.

...wait a moment...there *was* something left. Up there, just where the roots met...

Thank heavens; the thing was odd after all!

Oh happy day!

(pop)

*She loves me!*

# Descendant

am down, fallen as far as I am going to. Outwardly, I am just something on the surface, a body in a suit. Inwardly…
Everything is difficult. I hurt.

I feel better now. This is the third day. All I recall of the other two is that they were there; I don't remember any details. I haven't been getting better steadily, either, as what happened yesterday is even more blurred than the day before, the day of the fall.

I think I had the idea then that I was being born. A primitive, old-fashioned, almost animal birth; bloody and messy and dangerous. I took part and watched at the same time; I was the born and the birthing, and when, suddenly, I felt I could move, I jerked upright, trying to sit up and wipe my eyes, but my gloved hands hit the visor, centimetres in front of my eyes, and I fell back, raising dust. I blacked out.

Now it is the third day, however, and the suit and I are in better shape, ready to move off, start travelling.

I am sitting on a big rough rock in a boulderfield halfway up a long, gently sloping escarpment. I think it's a scarp. It might be the swell towards the lip of the big crater, but I haven't spotted any obvious secondaries that might belong to a hole in the direction of the rise, and there's no evidence of strata overflip.

Probably an escarpment then, and not too steep on the other side, I hope. I prepare myself by thinking of the way ahead before I actually start walking. I suck at the little tube near my chin and draw some thin, acidic stuff into my mouth. I swallow with an effort.

The sky here is bright pink. It is mid-morning, and there

are only two stars visible on normal sight. With the external glasses tinted and polarized I can just see thin wispy clouds, high up. The atmosphere is still, down at this level, and no dust moves. I shiver, bumping inside the suit, as though the vacuous loneliness bruised me. It was the same the first day, when I thought the suit was dead.

"Are you ready to set off?" the suit says. I sigh and get to my feet, dragging the weight of the suit up with me for a moment before it, tiredly, flexes too.

"Yes. Let's get moving."

We set off. It is my turn to walk. The suit is heavy, my side aches monotonously, my stomach feels empty. The boulder-field stretches on into the edges of the distant sky.

I don't know what happened, which is annoying, though it wouldn't make any difference if I did know. It wouldn't have made any difference when it happened, either, because there was no time for me to do anything. It was a surprise: an ambush.

Whatever got us must have been very small or very far away, otherwise we wouldn't be here, still alive. If the module had taken any standard-sized warhead full on there would be only radiation and atoms left; probably not an intact molecule. Even a near miss would have left nothing recognizable to the unaided human eye. Only something tiny—perhaps not a warhead at all but just something moving fast—or a more distant miss, would leave wreckage.

I must remember that, hold on to that. However bad I may feel, I am still alive, when there was every chance that I would never get this far, even as a cinder, let alone whole and thinking and still able to walk.

But damaged. Both of us damaged. I am injured, but so is the suit, which is worse, in some ways.

It is running mostly on external power, soaking up the weak sunlight as best it can, but so inefficiently that it has to rest at night, when both of us have to sleep. Its communications and AG are wrecked, and the recycle and medical units are badly damaged too. All that and a tiny leak we can't find. I'm frightened.

It says I have internal bruising and I shouldn't be walking, but we talked it over and agreed that our only hope is to walk, to head in roughly the right direction and hope we're seen by the base we were heading for originally, in the module. The base is a thousand kilometres south of the northern ice cap. We came down north of the equator, but just how far north, we don't know. It's going to be a long walk, for both of us.

"How do you feel now?"

"Fine," the suit replies.

"How far do you think we'll get today?"

"Maybe twenty kilometres."

"That's not very much."

"You're not very well. We'll do better once you heal. You were quite ill."

Quite ill. There are still some little bits of sickness and patches of dried blood within the helmet, where I can see them. They don't smell any more, but they don't look very pleasant either. I'll try cleaning them up again tonight.

I am worried that, apart from anything else, the suit isn't being completely honest with me. It says it thinks our chances are fifty-fifty, but I suspect it either doesn't have any idea at all, or knows things are worse than it's telling me. This is what comes of having a smart suit. But I asked for one; it was my choice, so I can't complain. Besides, I might have died if the suit hadn't been as bright as it is. It got the two of us down here, out of the wrecked module and down through the thin atmosphere while I was still unconscious from the explosion. A standard suit might have done almost as well, but that probably wouldn't have been enough; it was a close run thing even as it was.

My legs hurt. The ground is fairly level, but occasionally I have to negotiate small ridges and areas of corrugated ground. My feet are sore too, but the pain in my legs worries me more.

I don't know if I'll be able to keep going all day, which is what the suit expects.

"How far did we come yesterday?"

"Thirty-five kilometres."

The suit walked all of that, carrying me like a dead weight. It got up and walked, clasping me inside it so I wouldn't bump around, and marched off, the wispy remains of its crippled emergency photopanels dragging over the dusty ground behind it like the wings of some strange, damaged insect.

Thirty-five klicks. I haven't done a tenth of that yet.

I'll just have to keep going. I can't disappoint it. I'd be letting the suit down. It has done so well to get us here in one piece, and it walked all that long way yesterday, supporting me while I was still rolling my eyes and drooling, mumbling about walking in a dream and being the living dead...so I can't let it down. If I fail I harm us both, lessening the suit's chances of survival, too.

The slope goes on. The ground is boringly uniform, always the same rusty brown. It frightens me that there is so little variety, so little sign of life. Sometimes we see a stain on a rock that might be plant life, but I can't tell, and the suit doesn't know because most of its external eyes and tactiles were burned out in the fall, and its analyzer is in no better condition than the AG or the transceiver. The suit's briefing on the planet didn't include a comprehensive Ecology, so we don't even know in theory whether the discolourations could be plants. Maybe we are the only life here, maybe there's nothing living or thinking for thousands and thousands of kilometres. The thought appals me.

"What are you thinking about?"

"Nothing," I tell it.

"Talk. You should talk to me."

But what is there to say? And why should I talk anyway?

I suppose it wants to make me talk so I'll forget the steady march, the tramp-tramp of my feet a couple of centimetres away from the ochre soil of this barren place.

I remember that when I was still in shock, and delirious, on the first day, I thought I stood outside us both and saw the suit open itself, letting my precious, fouled air out into the thin atmosphere, and I watched me dying in the airless cold, then saw the suit slowly, tiredly haul me out of itself, stiff and naked, a reptile-skin reverse, a chrysalis negative. It left me scrawny and nude and pathetic on the dusty ground and walked away, lightened and empty.

And maybe I'm still afraid it will do that, because together we might both die, but the suit, I'm fairly sure, could make it by itself quite easily. It could sacrifice me to save itself. It's the sort of thing a lot of humans would do.

"Mind if I sit down?" I say, and collapse onto a large boulder before the suit can reply.

"What hurts?" it asks.

"Everything. Mostly my legs and my feet."

"It'll take a few days for your feet to harden and your muscles to tone up. Rest when you feel like it. There's no sense in pushing yourself too hard."

"Hmm," I say. I want it to argue. I want it to tell me to stop whining and keep walking...but it doesn't want to play. I look down at my dangling legs. The suit's surface is blackened and covered in tiny pits and scars. Some hair-fine filaments wave, tattered and charred. My suit. I've had the thing for over a century and I've hardly used it. The brain's spent most of its time plugged into the main house unit back home, living at an added level of vicariousness. Even on holidays, I've spent most of my time on board ship, rather than venture out into hostile environments.

Well, we're sure as shit in a hostile environment now. All we have to do is walk halfway round an airless planet, overcome any and all obstacles in our way, and if the place we're heading for still exists, and if the suit's systems don't pack up completely, and if we don't get picked off by whatever destroyed the module, and if we aren't blown away by our own people, we're saved.

"Do you feel like going on now?"

"What?"

"We'd better be on our way, don't you think?"

"Oh. Yes. All right." I lower myself to the desert floor. My feet ache intensely for a while, but as I start to walk the pain ebbs. The slope looks just the way it did kilometres back. I am already breathing deeply.

I have a sudden and vivid image of the base as it might be, as it probably is: a vast, steaming crater, ripped out of the planet during the same attack that downed us. But even if that is the reality, we agreed it still makes sense to head there; rescuers or reinforcements will go there first. We have a better chance of being picked up there than anywhere else. Anyway, there was no module wreckage to stay beside on the ground; it was travelling so fast it burned up, even in this thin atmosphere, the way we very nearly did.

I still have a vague hope we'll be spotted from space, but I guess that's not likely now. Anything left intact up there is probably looking outwards. If we'd been noticed when we fell, or spotted on the surface, we'd have been picked up by now, probably only hours after we hit the dirt. They can't know we're here, and we can't get in touch with them. So all we can do is walk.

The rock and stones are getting gradually smaller.

I walk on.

It's night. I can't sleep.

The stars are spectacular, but no solace. I am cold, too, which doesn't help. We are still on the slope; we travelled a little over sixteen kilometres today. I hope we'll come to the lip of the escarpment tomorrow, or at least to some sort of change in the landscape. Several times today, while I walked, I had the impression that for all my effort, we weren't moving anywhere. Everything is so uniform.

Damn my human-basic ancestry. My side and belly are hurting badly. My legs and feet held out better than I expected, but my injuries torment me. My head hurts as well. Normally, the suit would pump me full of painkiller, relaxants or a sleeping draught, and whatever it is helps your muscles to build up and your body to repair itself. My body can't do those things for itself, the way most people's can, so I'm at the mercy of the suit.

It says its recycler is holding out. I don't like to tell it, but the thin gruel it's dispensing tastes disgusting. The suit says it is still trying to track down the site of the leak; no progress so far.

I have my arms and legs inside now. I'm glad, because this lets me scratch. The suit lies with its arms clipped into the sides and opened into the torso section, the legs together and melded, and the chest expanded to give me room. Meanwhile the carbon dioxide frosts outside and the stars shine steadily.

I scratch and scratch. Something else more altered humans wouldn't have to do. I can't make itches go away just by thinking. It isn't very comfortable in here. Usually it is; warm and cosy and pleasant, every chemical whim of the encased body catered for; a little womb to curl up in and dream. The inner lining can no longer alter the way it used to, so it stays quite hard, and feels—and smells—sweaty. I can smell the sewage system. I scratch my backside and turn over.

Stars. I stare at them, trying to match their unblinking gaze through the hazy, scratched surface of the helmet visor.

I put my arm back into the suit's and unclip. I reach round onto the top of the blown-out chest and feel in the front pack's pocket, taking out my antique still camera.

"What are you doing?"

"Going to take a photograph. Play me some music. Anything."

"All right." The suit plays me music from my youth while I point the camera at the stars. I clip the arm back and pass the camera through the chest lock. The camera is very cold; my breath mists on it. The viewer half unrolls, then jams. I tease it out with my nails, and it stays. The rest of the mechanism is working; my star pictures are fine, and, switching to some of the older magazines from the stock, they come up bright and

clear too. I look at the pictures of my home and friends on
the orbital, and feel—as I listen to the old, nostalgia-inducing
music—a mixture of comfort and sadness. My vision blurs.

I drop the camera and its screen snaps shut; the camera
rolls away underneath me. I raise myself up painfully, retrieve
it, unroll the screen again and go on looking back through old
photographs until I fall asleep.

I wake up.

The camera lies beside me, switched off. The suit is quiet.
I can hear my heart beat.

I drift back to sleep eventually.

Still night. I stay awake looking at the stars through the scarred
visor. I feel as rested as I ever will, but the night here is almost
twice standard, and I'll just have to get used to it. Neither of
us can see well enough to be able to travel safely at night,
besides which I still need to sleep, and the suit can't store
enough energy during the hours of sunlight to use for walking in the darkness; its internal power source produces barely
enough continuous energy to crawl with, and the light falling
on its photopanels provides a vital supplement. Thankfully,
the clouds here never seem to amount to much; an overcast
day would leave me doing all the work whether it was my
turn or not.

I unroll the camera screen, then think.

"Suit?"

"What?" it says quietly.

"The camera has a power unit."

"I thought of that. It's very weak, and anyway the power
systems are damaged beyond the junction point for another
source of internal energy. I can't think of a way of patching it
into the external radiation system, either."

"We can't use it?"

"We can't use it. Just look at your pictures."

I look at the pictures.

There's no doubt about it; education or not, once you've been born and brought up on an O you never quite adjust to a planet. You get agoraphobic; you feel you are about to be sent spinning off, flying away into space, picked up and sent screaming and bawling out to the naked stars. You somehow sense that vast, wasteful bulk underneath you, warping space itself and self-compressing, soil-solid or still half-molten, quivering in its creaky, massy press, and you; stuck, perched here on the outside, half-terrified that despite all you know you'll lose your grip and go wheeling and whirling and wailing away.

This is our birthplace though, this is what we deserted long ago. This is where we used to live, on balls of dust and rock like this. This is our home town from before we felt the itch of wanderlust, the sticks we inhabited before we ran away from home, the cradle where we were infected with the crazy breath of the place's vastness like a metal wind inside our love-struck heads; just stumbled on the scale of what's around and tripped out drunk on starlike possibilities...

I find that I'm staring at the stars, my eyes wide and burning. I shake myself, tear my sight away from the view outside, turn back to the camera.

I look at a group photograph from the orbital. People I knew; friends, lovers, relations, children; all standing in the sunlight of a late summer's day, outside the main building. Recalled names and faces and voices, smells and touches. Behind them, almost finished, is—as it was then—the new wing. Some of the wood we used to build it still lies in the garden, white and dark brown on the green. Smiles. The smell of sawdust and the feel of pushing a plane; hardened skin on my hands and the sight and sound of the planed wood curling from the blade.

Tears again. How can I help but be sentimental? I didn't expect all of this, back then. I can't cope with the distance between us all now, that awful gap of slow years.

I flick through other pictures; general views of the orbital, its fields and towns and seas and mountains. Maybe everything can be seen as a symbol in the end; perhaps with our limited grasp we can't help but find similarities, talismans...but that inward facing plate of orbital looks false to me now, down here, so far away and lonely. This globe of ordinary, soft, accidental planet seems the cutting edge and the flat knife of twinned adamantine thoroughness, our clever, efficient little orbitals, lacking that fundamental reality.

I wish I could sleep. I want to sleep and forget about everything, but I can't, tired though I still am. The suit can't help me there, either. I don't even remember dreaming, as though that facility, too, is damaged.

Maybe I'm the artificial one, not the suit, which doesn't try to pretend. People have said I'm cold, which hurt me; which still hurts me. All I can do is feel what I can and tell myself it's all anyone can ask of me.

I turn over painfully, face away from the treacherous stars. I close my eyes and my mind to their remindful study, and try to sleep.

"Wake up"

I feel very sleepy, the rhythms all wrong, tired again.

"Time to go; come on."

I come to, rubbing my eyes, breathing through my mouth to get rid of the stale taste in it. The dawn looks cold and perfect, very thin and wide through this inhospitable covering of gas. And the slope is still here, of course.

It's the suit's turn to walk, so I can rest on. We redeploy the legs and arms again, the chest deflates. The suit stands up and starts walking, gripping me round the calves and waist, taking the bulk of my weight off my throbbing feet.

The suit walks faster than I do. It reckons it is only twenty per cent stronger than the average human. Something of a come-down for it. Even having to walk must be galling for it (if it feels galled).

If only the AG worked. We'd do the whole trip in a day. One day.

We stride out over the sloped plain, heading for the edge. The stars disappear slowly, one by one, washed out of the wide skies by the sunlight. The suit gains a little speed as the light falls harder on its trailed photopanels. We stop and squat for a moment, inspecting a discoloured rock; it is just possible, if we find an oxide of some sort...but the stone holds no more trapped oxygen than the rest, and we move on.

"When and if we get back, what will happen to you?"

"Because I'm damaged?" the suit says. "I imagine they'll just throw the body away, it's so badly damaged."

"You'll get a new one?"

"Yes, of course."

"A better one?"

"I expect so."

"What will they keep? Just the brain?"

"Plus about a metre of secondary column and a few subunits."

I want us to get there. I want us to be found. I want to live.

We come to the edge of the escarpment about mid-morning. Even though I am not walking I feel very tired and sleepy, and my appetite has disappeared. The view ought to be impressive, but I'm only aware that it's a long, difficult way down. The escarpment lip is crumbly and dangerous, cut with many runnels and channels, which lower down become steep, shadowy ravines separating sharp-edged ridges and jagged spires. Scree spreads out beyond, far below, in the landscape at the cliff's foot; it is the colour of old, dried blood.

I am suitably depressed.

We sit on a rock and rest before making our way down. The horizon is very clear and sharp. There are mountains in the far distance, and many broad, shallow channels on the wide plain that lies between the mountains and us.

I don't feel well. My guts ache continually and breathing deeply hurts too, as though I've broken a rib. I think it is just the taste of the recycler's soup that is putting me off eating, but I'm not certain. There are a few stars in the sky.

"We couldn't glide down, could we?" I ask the suit. That's how we got through the atmosphere, after all. The suit used the minuscule amount of AG it had left, and somehow got the tattered photopanel sheet to function as a parachute.

"No. The AG is almost certain to fail completely next time we try it, and the parachute trick...we'd need too much space, too much drop to ensure deployment."

"We have to climb?"

"We have to climb."

"All right, we'll climb." We get up, approach the edge.

Night again. I am exhausted. So tired, but I cannot sleep. My side is tender to the touch and my head throbs unbearably. It took us the whole afternoon and evening to get down here to the plains, and we both had to work at it. We nearly fell, once. A good hundred-metre drop with just some flakes of slatey stone to hold on to until the suit kicked a foothold. Somehow we made it down without snagging and tearing further the photopanels. More good luck than skill, probably. Every muscle seems to hurt. I'm finding it hard to think straight. All I want to do is twist and turn and try to find a comfortable way to lie.

I don't know how much of this I can take. This is going to go on for a hundred days or more, and even if the still undiscovered leak doesn't kill me I feel like I'm going to die of exhaustion. If only they were looking for us. Somebody walking in a suit on a planet sounds hard to find, but shouldn't be really. The place is barren, homogeneous, dead and motionless. We must be the only movement, the only life, for hundreds of kilometres at least. To our level of technology we ought to stand out like a boulder in the dust, but either they aren't looking or there's nobody left to look.

But if the base still exists, they must see us eventually, mustn't they? The sats can't spend all their time looking outwards, can they? They must have some provision for spotting enemy landings. Could we have just slipped through? It doesn't seem possible.

I look at my photographs again. They appear a hundred at a time on the viewer. I press one and it blooms to fill the little screen with its memories.

I rub my head and wonder how long my hair will grow. I have a silly but oddly frightening vision of my hair growing so long it chokes me, filling the helmet and the suit and cutting out the light, finally asphyxiating me. I've heard that your hair goes on growing after you die, and your nails too. I wonder that—despite one or two of the photographs, and their associated memories—I haven't felt sexually aroused yet.

I curl up, foetal. I am a little naked planet of my own, reduced to the primitive within my own stale envelope of gas. A tiny moonlet of this place, on a very low, slow, erratic orbit.

What am I doing here?

It's as if I drifted into this situation. I didn't ever think about fighting or doing anything risky at all, not until the war came along. I agreed it was necessary, but that seemed obvious; everybody thought so, everybody I knew, anyway. And volunteering, agreeing to take part; that too seemed... natural. I knew I might die, but I was prepared to risk that; it was almost romantic. Somehow it never occurred to me it might entail privation and suffering. Am I as stupid as those throughout history—those I've always despised and pitied—who've marched off to war, heads full of noble notions and expectations of easy glory, only to die screaming and torn in the mud?

I thought I was different. I thought I knew what I was doing.

"What are you thinking about?" the suit asks.

"Nothing."

"Oh."

"Why are *you* here?" I ask it. "Why did you agree to come with me?"

The suit—officially as smart as me, and with similar rights—could have gone its own way if it wanted. It didn't have to come to war.

"Why shouldn't I come with you?"

"But what's in it for you?"

"What's in it for *you?*"

"But I'm human; I can't help feeling like this. I want to know what you think the machines' excuse is."

"Oh, come on; you're a machine too. We're both *systems*, we're both matter with sentience. What makes you think we have more choice than you in the way we think? Or that you have so little? We're all programmed. We all have our inheritance. You have rather more than us, and it's more chaotic, that's all."

There is a saying that we provide the machines with an end, and they provide us with the means. I have a fleeting impression the suit is about to trot out this hoary adage.

"Do you really *care* what happens in the war?" I ask it.

"Of course," it says, with what could almost be a laugh in its voice. I lie back and scratch. I look at the camera.

"I've got an idea," I tell it. "How about I find a very bright picture and wave it about now, in the dark?"

"You can try it, if you want." The suit doesn't sound very encouraging. I try it anyway, then my arm gets tired waving the camera around. I leave it propped up against a rock, shining into space. It looks very lonely and strange, that picture of a sunny orbital day, sky and clouds and glittering water, bright hulls and tall sails, fluttering pennants and dashing spray, in this dead and dusty darkness. It isn't all that bright though; I suspect reflected starlight isn't much weaker. It would be easy to miss, and they don't seem to be looking anyway.

"I wonder what happens to us all in the end," I yawn, sleepy at last.

"I don't know. We'll just have to wait and see."

"Won't that be fun," I murmur, and say no more.

The suit says this is day twenty.

We are in the foothills on the far side of the mountains we saw in the distance from the escarpment. I am still alive.

The pressure in the suit is reduced to slow down the loss rate from the leak, which the suit has decided is not a hole as such, but increased osmosis from several areas where too much of the outer layers ablated when we were falling. I am breathing pure oxygen now, which lets us bring down the pressure significantly. It might be coincidence, but the food from the recycler tube tastes better since we switched to pure gas.

There is a dull ache all the time from my belly, but I am learning to live with it. I've stopped caring, I think. I'll live or I'll die, but worrying and complaining won't improve my chances. The suit isn't sure what to make of this. It doesn't know whether I have given up hope or just become blasé about the whole thing. I feel no guilt at keeping it guessing.

I lost the camera.

I was trying, eight days ago, to take a photograph of a strange, anthropomorphous rock formation in the high mountains, when the camera slipped from my fingers and fell into a crevice between two great boulders. The suit seemed almost as unhappy as I was; normally it could have lifted either of those rocks into the air, but even together the two of us couldn't budge either of them.

My feet are hard and calloused, now, which makes walking a lot easier. I am becoming hardened generally. I'll be a better person when I come out of this, I'm sure. The suit makes dubious noises when I suggest this.

I've seen some lovely sunsets recently. They must have been there all the time, but I didn't notice them. I make a point of watching them now, sitting up to observe the sweep and trace of trembling, planetary air and the high clouds wisping and curling, coming and going, levels and layers of the wrapping atmosphere shifting through its colours and turning like smooth, silent shells.

There is a small moon I hadn't noticed either. I put the external glasses on as high as they will go and sit looking at its grey face, when I can find it. I rebuked the suit for not reminding me the planet had a moon. It told me it hadn't thought it was important.

The moon is pale and fragile looking, and pocked.

I have taken to singing songs to myself. This annoys the suit intensely, and sometimes I pretend that's one of the major rewards of such vocal self-indulgence. Sometimes I think it really is, too. They are very poor songs, because I am not very good at making them up, and I have a terrible memory for other people's. The suit insists my voice is flat as well, but I think it's just being mean. Once or twice it has retaliated by playing music very loudly through my headphones, but I just sing louder and it gives in. I try to get it to sing along with me, but it sulks.

*"Oh once there was a space-man,*
*And a happy man was he.*
*Flew through the big G,*
*And really saw it all, yes,*
*But then one day, I'm afraid,*
*He happened to trip up,*
*Stumbled on a pla-anet*
*And landed in the dirt.*

*It wouldn't really have been so bad,*
*But the worst was yet to come;*
*His one and only companion*
*Was a suit that da da dum.*
*The suit it was a shit-bag*
*And thought the man a lout,*
*And what it really wanted*
*Was to be inside-out.*

*(chorus:)*
*Inside-out, inside-out, inside inside-out,*
*Inside-out, inside-out, inside inside-out!"*

And so on. There are others, but they are mostly to do with sex, and so fairly boring; colourful but monotonous.

My hair is growing. I have a thin beard.

I have started masturbating, though only every few days. It is all recycled, of course. I claim the suit as my lover. It is not amused.

I miss my comforts, but at least sex can be partially recreated, whereas all the rest seem unreal, no more than dreams. I have started dreaming. Usually it is the same dream; I am on a cruise of some sort, somewhere. I don't know what form of transport I'm on, but somehow I know it's moving. It might be a ship, or a seaship, or an airship, or a train...I don't know. All that happens is that I walk down a fleecy corridor, passing plants and small pools. Some sort of scenery is going by outside, when I can see outside, but I'm not paying very much attention. It might be a planet seen from space, or mountains, or desert, it might even be underwater; I don't care. I wave to some people I know. I am eating something savoury to tide me over to dinner, and I have a towel over my shoulder; I think I'm going for a swim. The air is sweet and I hear some very soft and beautiful music which I almost recognize, coming from a cabin. Wherever, whatever it is I am in, it is travelling very smoothly and quietly, without sound or vibration or fuss; secure.

I'll appreciate all that if I ever see it again. I'll know then what it is to feel so safe, so pampered, so unafraid and confident.

I never get anywhere in that dream. I'm always simply walking, each and every time I have it. It is always the same, always as sweet; I always start and finish in the same place, everything is always the same; predictable and comforting. Everything is very sharp and clear. I miss nothing.

Day thirty. The mountains way behind us, and me—us—walking along the top of an ancient lava tunnel. I'm looking for a break in the roof because I think it'll be fun to walk along within the tunnel itself—it looks big enough to walk inside. The suit says we aren't heading in exactly the right direction for the base, following the tunnel, but I reckon we're close enough. It indulges me. I deserve to be indulged; I can't curl up like a little ball at night any more. The suit decided we were losing too much oxygen each time we melded the limbs and inflated the suit at night, so we've stopped doing that. I hated feeling trapped, and unable to scratch, at first, but now I don't mind so much. Now I have to sleep with my legs in its legs and my arms in its arms.

The lava tunnel curves away in the wrong direction. I stand looking at it as it wiggles away into the distance, up a great slope to a distant, extinct shield volcano. Wrong way, damn it.

"Let's get down and head in the right direction, shall we?" the suit says.

"Oh, all right," I grumble. I get down. I'm sweating. I wipe my head inside the helmet, rubbing it up and down, like an animal scratching. "I'm sweating," I tell it. "Why are you letting me sweat? I shouldn't be sweating. You shouldn't be letting me sweat. You must be letting your attention wander. Come on; do your job."

"Sorry," the suit says, in an unpleasant tone. I think it should take my comfort a little more seriously. That's what it's there for, after all.

"If you want me to get out and walk, I will," I tell it.

"That won't be necessary."

I wish it would suggest a rest. I feel weak and dizzy again, and I could feel the suit doing most of the work as we got down from the roof of the lava tunnel. The pain in my guts is back. We start walking over the rubble-covered plain once more. I feel like talking.

"Tell me, suit, don't you wonder if it's all worth it?"

"If what's all worth what?" it says, and I can hear that condescending tone in its voice again.

"You know; living. Is it worth all the...bother?"

"No."

"*No?*"

"No, I don't ever wonder about it."

"Why not?" I'm keeping my questions short as we walk, conserving energy and breath.

"I don't need to wonder about that. It's not important."

"Not *important*?"

"It's an irrelevant question. We live; that's enough."

"Oh. That easy, huh?"

"Why not?"

"Why?"

The suit is silent after that. I wait for it to say something, but it doesn't. I laugh, wave both our arms about. "I mean, what's it all about, suit? What does it all mean?"

"What colour is the wind? How long is a piece of string?"

I have to think about that. "What's *string*?" I have to ask finally, suspecting I've missed something.

"Never mind. Keep walking."

Sometimes I wish I could see the suit. It's weird, now that I think about it, not being able to see who I'm talking to. Just this hollow voice, not unlike my own, sounding in the space between the inside of my helmet and the outside of my skull. I would prefer a face to look at, or even just a single thing to fix my attention on.

If I still had the camera I could take a photograph of us both. If there was water here I could gaze at our reflection.

The suit is my shape, extended, but its mind isn't mine; it's independent. This perplexes me, though I suppose it must make sense. But I'm glad I chose the full 1.0 intelligence version; the standard 0.1 type would have been no company at all. Perhaps my sanity is measured by the placing of a decimal point.

Night. It is the fifty-fifth night. Tomorrow will be the fifty-sixth day.

How am I? Difficult to say. My breathing has become laboured, and I'm sure I've become thinner. My hair is long now and my beard quite respectable, if a little patchy. Hairs fall out, and I have to squirm and pull to get an arm into the body of the suit to poke the hairs into the waste unit each night, or they itch. I am woken up at night by the pain inside me. It is like a little life itself, pawing and scraping to get out.

Sometimes I dream a lot, sometimes not at all. I have given up singing. The land goes on. I had forgotten planets were so *big*. This one's smaller than standard, and it still seems to go on and on without end. I feel very cold, and the stars make me cry.

I am tormented by erotic dreams, and can do nothing about them. They are similar to the old dream, of walking on the ship or the seaship or whatever it is...only in this dream the people around me are naked, and caressing each other, and I am on my way to my lover...but when I wake up and try to masturbate, nothing happens. I try and try, but I only exhaust myself. Perhaps if the dream was more powerfully erotic, more imaginative...but it stays the same.

I've been thinking about the war a lot recently, and I think I've decided it's wrong. We are defeating ourselves in waging it, will destroy ourselves by winning it. All our statistics and assumptions mean less the more they seem to tell. We surrender, in our militance, not to one enemy but to all we've ever fought, within ourselves. We should not be involved, we ought not to do a thing; we've gambled our fine irony for a mechanistic piety, and the faith we fight's our own.

Get out, stay out, keep clear.

Did I say that?

I thought the suit said something there. I'm not sure. Sometimes I think it's talking to me all the time when I'm asleep. It might even be talking to me all the time when I'm awake, too, but it's only occasionally that I hear it. I think it's mimicking me, trying to sound the way I sound. Perhaps it wants to drive me mad, I don't know.

Sometimes I don't know which of us has said something.

I shiver and try to turn over in the suit, but I can't. I wish I wasn't here. I wish all this hadn't happened. I wish it was all a dream, but like the colours of the earth and air, it's too consistent.

I feel very cold, and the stars make me cry.

*"Inside-out, inside-out, inside inside-out,*
*Inside-out, inside-out, inside inside-out!"*

"Shut up!"

"Oh, you're talking to me at last."

"I said *shut up!*"

"But I wasn't saying anything."

"You were singing!"

"I don't sing. You were singing."

"Don't lie! Don't you dare lie to me! You were singing!"

"I assure you—"

"You were! I heard you!"

"You're shouting. Calm down. We still have a long way to go. We shan't get there if you—"

"Don't you tell me to shut up!"

"I didn't. You told me to shut up."

"What?"

"I said—"

"What did you say?"

"I—"

"What? What did—who is that?"

"If you'll ju—"

"Who are you? Who *are you*? Oh no, please..."

"Look, ca—"

"No, please..."

"What?"

"...please..."

"*What?*"

"...please...please...please...please..."

I don't know what day this is. I don't know where I am or how far I've come or how far there is still to go.

Sane now. There never was any suit voice. I made it all up; it was my own voice all the time. Some state I must have been in to imagine all that, to be so unable to cope with being down here, all alone, that I created somebody else to talk to, like some lonely kid with a friend nobody else can see. I believed in it when I thought I heard the voice, but I don't hear it any more. Even at its most blandly credible it was just the flat calm of insanity. Temporary, fortunately. Everything is.

I don't look at the stars any more, in case they start talking to me too.

Maybe the base is at the core. Maybe I am just walking round it and can never get any closer to it.

My limbs move on their own now; automatic, programmed. I hardly need to think. Everything is as it should be.

We don't need the machines, any more than they need us. We just think we need them. They don't matter. Only they need themselves. Of course a smart suit would have ditched me to save itself; we didn't build them to resemble ourselves, but that's the way it works out, in the end.

We created something a little closer to perfection than our-selves; maybe that's the only way to progress. Let them try to do the same. I doubt they can, so they will always be less as well as more than us. It's all just a sum, a whispered piece of figuring lost in the empty blizzards of white noise howling through the universe, brief oasis in an infinite desert, a freak bit of working-out in which we have transcended ourselves, and they are only the remainder.

Going mad inside a space-suit, indeed.

I think I passed the place where the base used to be some time ago, but there was nothing there. I am still walking. I'm not sure I know how to stop.

I am a satellite; they, too, only stay up by forever falling forward.

The suit is dead around me, burned and scarred and black-ened and lifeless. I don't know how I could have dreamed it was alive. The very thought makes me shiver, inside here.

A guard drone's knife missile saw the figure skylining about five kilometres away, on a low ridge. The little missile sized the object up carefully, not moving from its crevice in the rocks. It triangulated from the eyes on its outboard monofilament warps, then rose slowly from its hiding place until it was in line of sight with a scout missile lodged on a cliff ten kilometres behind it. It flashed a brief signal, and received a relayed reply from its distant drone.

The drone was there in a few minutes, taking a wide curve round the suspicious figure. It shook other missiles free as it went, deploying them in a ring around the potential target.

What to do? The drone had to make up its own mind. The base wasn't transmitting while whatever had hit the last incoming module was still hanging around. It had been a long wait, but they'd survived so far, and the big guns should be arriving soon.

The drone watched the figure as it skidded and slid down the scree beneath the ridge, leaving a hazy trail of dust behind it. It got to the bottom, then started walking across the wide gravel basin, seemingly oblivious to all the attention it was attracting.

The drone sent a knife missile closer to the object. The missile floated up from behind, monitoring weak electromagnetic emissions, tried to communicate but received no reply, then darted round in front of the figure, and lasered its drone the view it had of the scarred suit front.

The figure stopped, stood still. It raised one hand, as though waving at the small missile hovering a few metres in front of it. The drone came closer, high above, scanning. Finally, satisfied, it swooped from the sky and stopped a metre in front of the figure, which pointed at the black mess of the communication unit on its chest. Then it gestured to the side of its helmet and tapped at the visor. The drone dipped once in a nod, then floated forward and pressed gently up against the visor of the helmet, vibrating the speech through.

"We know who you are. What happened?"

"He was alive when we got down, but I had no medics left. Ablation caused a slow oxygen leak and eventually the recycler packed up. There was nothing I could do."

"You walked all this way?"

"From near the equator."

"When did he die?"

"Thirty-four days ago."

"Why didn't you ditch the body? You'd have been quicker."

The suit made a shrugging movement. "Call it sentiment."

"Climb aboard. I'll take you to an entrance."

"Thank you."

The drone lowered to waist height. The suit pulled itself up onto the top of the drone and sat there.

The body, bouncing slackly inside the suit, was still quite well preserved, though dehydration had stretched the skin and made it darker. The teeth were displayed grinning knowingly at the barren world, and the skull was arched back on the locked upper vertebrae, upright and triumphant.

"You all right up there?" the drone shouted through the fabric of the suit. The suit nodded stiffly to the eye of an accompanying knife missile.

"Yes. Everything's a little difficult though." It pointed at the scarred, burned surface of its body. "I hurt."

# Cleaning Up

The first Gift fell onto a pig farm in New England. It popped into existence five metres above a ramshackle outhouse, dropped through the roof, bounced off a cistern and demolished a wheel-less tractor driving a band saw.

Bruce Losey came running out of the house clutching his sporting carbine and ready to blast any interloper to Kingdom Come. All he found was what looked like a gigantic bundle of peacock feathers on top of his tractor, which was lying on its side leaking fuel and looking like it would never work again. Bruce looked up through the hole in the roof and spat into a pile of cut logs, "Goddamned S.S.T.s."

He tried to shift the object that had bust up his tractor, smashed his roof and dented his cistern, but leapt away when it burned his hands. He went back to the house watching the sky warily, and called the police.

Cesare Borges, head of the mighty Industrial Military Combines Corporation, sat in his office reading a fascinating article called *Prayer: A Guide to Investment?* The office intercom buzzed.

"What?"

"Professor Feldman to see you, sir."

"Who?"

"A Professor Feldman, sir."

"Oh yeah?"

"Yes, sir. He says he has the results of the preliminary development work on...," there was some talking Cesare didn't catch, "...on the Alternative Resources Project."

"The what?"

"The Alternative Resources Project, sir. It was set up last year, it seems. The professor has been waiting for some time, sir."

"I'll see him later," Cesare said, clicking the intercom off and going back to the *Reader's Digest.*

"Hell, *I* don't know what it is."

"I think it fell off an S.S.T."

The patrolman rubbed his chin. The other cop was poking a stick at the bundle lying across the old tractor. The thing was about three metres long and one in diameter, and whatever it was its colours kept shifting and changing, and whenever anything touched it, it got hot. The tip of the stick smoked.

"Who should we tell about this anyway?" said the cop with the stick. He wanted to have this cleared up as quickly as possible and get away from the smell of pigs coming from the barn across the yard.

"I guess...the F.A.A.," said the other, "or maybe the Air Force. I dunno." He took off his cap and fiddled with the badge, breathing on it and polishing it on his sleeve.

"Well I'm claiming compensation, whoever it belongs to," Bruce said as they went back to the house. "That's a lot of damage that thing's done. That'll cost a few bucks to set right. That tractor was nearly new, you know. I'm telling you; nowhere's safe now with those S.S.T.s."

"Hmm."

"Uh-huh."

"Hey," Bruce said, stopping and looking at the two cops with a worried expression on his face, "do you know if Liberia registers S.S.T.s?"

Professor Feldman sat in the outer-outer office in Cesare's suite at the top of the I.M.C.C. building in Manhattan and looked through the abstract of his report for about the eightieth time.

The secretary, a clean-cut young man with an IBM 9000 desk terminal and a M.23 submachine gun, had shrugged his shoulders sympathetically after he had at last been persuaded to call through to Cesare's office. The professor said he would just have to wait, and went back to his seat. There were seven other people waiting to see Cesare apart from himself. Two of them were Air Force generals and one was the foreign minister of an important developing country. They all looked nervous without their aides, who were kept in the outer-outer-outer office to avoid crowding. According to the others, they had been waiting there, seven or eight hours each day, five days a week, for at least the last three weeks.

This was the professor's first day.

The factory ship moved through space in one of the dust-rich arms of the main galaxy, its net-fields like great, invisible limbs stretched before it, gathering its harvest like a trawl and funnelling the ensnared material into the first-stage Transmuters.

In the mess of the Third Clean-Up Squad, things were going badly for Matriapoll Trasnegatherstoleken-iffregienthickissle, jnr. He had almost completed a full circuit of the room without touching the floor when a collapsible chair collapsed beneath him, and now he had to go back to the start and begin all over again with one paw tied behind his back. The other members of the Squad were making bets on where he would fall and screaming insults.

"7833 Matriapoll and Mates to briefing room fourteen!" blared the mess-room speaker.

Normally Matriapoll would have welcomed this interruption, but he was on top of the speaker trying to grab hold of a light fixture at the time, and the shock of the speaker suddenly bursting into life beneath him made him lose his grip, and he thumped down onto the floor to the accompaniment of hoots and laughter.

"Bastards," he said.

"Come on, Matty," chuckled his Mates, Oney and Twoey, their tiny, dextrous hands quickly untying his arm and dusting him down. They straightened his clothes and bustled out in front of him as Matriapoll paid what he owed to the others in the Squad and then left for the briefing room.

* * *

The Air Force didn't know what it was either, but it wasn't anything of theirs, they were sure of that. *They* certainly weren't going to be paying any compensation. But they decided to take the thing, just to see what it was.

The Air Force came in a big truck that didn't quite make the turn off the road onto the farm track, and knocked down a metre or two of fencing. Bruce said he'd sue.

They took the bundle away wrapped in asbestos.

At the Mercantsville Airbase they tried to find out what the object was, but apart from deducing that—from the way it felt—there was something inside the oddly-coloured outer covering, which now appeared like mother-of-pearl, they didn't make a great deal of progress.

Somebody in I.M.C.C. got to hear about the object and the Company offered to open it, or at least make a further attempt, if the Air Force would let them have it.

The Air Force thought about this. The mysterious bundle was resisting all attempts to open it or even see inside. They had tried metal tools, which melted; they tried oxy-acetylene torches, which disappeared into the mother-of-pearl covering without producing any noticeable effect; oxygen lances, which did no better; shaped-charge explosives, which shifted the whole thing across the floor of the hangar; and laser beams, which bounced off and frazzled the roof.

A few days later a truck left the Mercantsville base and made its way to the nearest I.M.C.C. laboratory.

Professor Feldman had started a series of chess games with the foreign minister. Two more people had arrived in the outer-outer office to wait. One of the generals had given up and left. Professor Feldman could see that he might have to wait quite a while before being granted an audience with Mr. Borges. He had a sinking feeling that by the time he got in to see the chief, all the problems in the world that the A.R.P. was supposed to help alleviate would have disappeared, one way or another.

The foreign minister wasn't very good at chess.

*   *   *

The scoutship warped its way through space.

Matriapoll picked what passed with his people for a nose and watched the show on the control-cabin screen. The show was extremely boring; yet another quiz programme where people answered questions that were far too easy and got prizes that were far too expensive, but Matriapoll kept watching because the hostesses who showed the prizes to the audience were beautiful. The green one in particular had the most superb trio of *phnysthens* he could recall seeing.

The show cut out suddenly and was replaced by a picture of stars. One star was ringed in red by the ship's computer.

"Is that where we're going?" said a little voice behind him.

"Yes," said Matriapoll to Twoey. The little animal curled its arm around his neck and peeped over his shoulder, rubbing its snout on his collar.

"That's where the Transporter's focused?"

"Right there, on the system's sun." Matty frowned. "Or at least that's where it's *meant* to be targeted."

Another Gift turned up in Kansas, another in Texas. One was seen from a drilling rig in the Gulf of Mexico, falling into the water. They still hadn't worked out how to open them. They tried bombarding them with light, radio, x and gamma rays and they tried ultrasonic equipment on it too. They did all the same things to the Kansas object and the Texas object, but none of them gave up any of their secrets.

Eventually they put the original bundle into a vacuum chamber. That didn't work either until they heated one side and froze the other. The thing peeled like a wrapper off candy, and for an instant the people outside the chamber were left gazing at something that looked like a cross between a suit of armour and a missile, before it blew up and caught fire.

They were left with a very odd pile of junk, but the *next* time...

\*   \*   \*

Cesare was on the phone.

"OK, I'm a busy man; there are a lot of people waiting to see me. What is it?"

The phone made noises. Cesare watched the Manhattan skyline, then he said, "Oh yeah?"

The phone made more noises. Cesare nodded. He inspected his fingernails and sighed.

While he was doing that, a general swinging on the end of a length of rope tied around his waist passed in front of Cesare's office window waving plans for a new high-altitude bomber. Cesare looked into the phone.

"What?"

The rope came back empty, and a sheaf of papers floated for a moment in front of the glass before the breeze caught them and took them away, drifting slowly down to the streets, eighty floors below.

"And it's just floating there? No engines? No noise? Nothing?"

The rope was hanging just outside the window, the remains of a poorly tied knot at the end.

"Anti-gravity? Sure."

Cesare put the phone down without another word. *I am surrounded by idiots*, he thought.

Gifts started popping into existence all over the place. Some were found in Europe, one in Australia, two in Africa, three in South America.

I.M.C.C had thirteen, eleven of them found in the USA and one each from South America and Africa. They found out how to open them without damaging the contents, and what they found were some very odd things indeed.

One kept trying to walk away on its five legs. It looked a little like a spider. Another just floated in mid-air without any apparent means of support. It vaguely resembled a type-writer with headlamps. Another was the size of a sub-compact automobile and tried to talk to everybody with blond hair in a language which appeared to consist mostly of grunts and wind-breaking noises. Yet another seemed to be a different size and shape every time you looked at it. All were very difficult to take apart, and the analysis of any bits that they did eventually succeed in removing didn't make sense.

Professor Feldman sat beside the Police Chief who was waiting to see Cesare to ask whether he knew anything about the Air Force general who had, it seemed, jumped to his death from the roof of the building a few days ago. The professor had been talking about this with the policeman, and was shocked to discover that it was the same general he had been waiting with up to a week ago. The other general, who was still there waiting, said he couldn't help in the investigation.

"Checkmate," Professor Feldman said, after eight moves.

"Are you sure?" said the foreign minister, leaning closer to inspect the board. Feldman was about to reply when the young secretary came over and tapped him on the shoulder.

"Professor Feldman?"

"Yes?"

"Would you like to go in? Mr. Borges will see you now."

The young secretary went back to his seat. The professor looked around at the others, aghast. They were glaring at him with that special contempt reserved by the envious for the undeserving. The remaining general sneered openly at him and glanced meaningfully down at the patchwork of ribbons that covered one side of his chest. The professor gathered up his papers in total silence and gave his lunchbox and magazines to the policeman. He pulled his tie straight and walked as steadily as he could to the door, still wondering why he had been summoned before people who had been waiting much longer than he had.

Cesare Borges straightened his tie, put the edition of *National Geographic* away, and emptied the small box containing the names of the rest of the people sitting in the outer-outer office into the waste-bin. Professor Feldman's slip of paper was marking Cesare's place in the magazine.

"Well?" he said when Professor Feldman walked into the room. Cesare motioned him to sit in a seat in front of the massive desk. Feldman sat down and cleared his throat. He took some papers and spread them deferentially on Cesare's desk.

"Well, sir, these are some of the projects we've been working on in this, the first phase of what I like to call—"

"What's this?" snorted Cesare, holding up a piece of paper with a drawing on it.

"That? That's...ah...that's a new design of mud-press for constructing bricks in a low-technology situation."

Cesare looked at him. He picked up another bit of paper. "And this?"

"That's a section through a new, low-cost, long-life toilet we've designed for when water is at a premium."

"You've spent two million of the firm's money designing a *john*?" Cesare said huskily.

"Well, sir, it's very important. It's just one component in a whole system of low-cost, high-use interdependent facilities which have been designed to be of facility in the Third World. Of course, the development costs will probably be recouped in production, though it was agreed that it would be very good for the overall image of the company and the associated universities if there was no actual profit component included in the eventual selling price."

"It was?" said Cesare.

The professor coughed nervously. "So I believe, sir. That was at the last shareholders' meeting. The grant for the project as a whole dates from then, although the preliminary viability study was first—"

"Just a minute," Cesare said, holding up one hand and putting the other to the buzzing intercom. "Yes?"

"Call on line two, sir."

Cesare picked up the phone. Feldman sat back and wondered what was going to happen. Cesare said, "Are you *sure*? And this could definitely be used? This had better be right. OK. Hold everything; I'm coming out there." He put down the phone and hit a button on the intercom set. "Get the helicopter and have the jet ready."

"Ah...Mr. Borges—" Professor Feldman began as Cesare opened a drawer in his desk and took out a travelling bag. Cesare held up one hand.

"Not now, doc; I got to move. Just wait in the outer-outer office until I send for you. I won't be long. So long."

With that he was gone, into his private elevator and on up to the roof to his private helicopter which would fly him to an I.M.C.C. airstrip where his private jet would be waiting. The young secretary came into the office and ushered Professor Feldman and his papers back out into the outer-outer office, where nobody talked to him and the foreign minister and the Police Chief were playing chequers on his chess board.

"Black Holes!" Matriapoll said loudly.

"What's wrong, Matty?" said Oney. The three of them were watching a complicated array of lights and screens in the control cabin. The system and surrounding space was shown diagrammatically, and a little red light had just appeared next to the third planet, counting out from the star.

"I'll tell you what's wrong," said Matriapoll, clicking his brows with annoyance. "That Transporter *is* out-of-order."

"It's not working, Matty?"

"It's working, but it isn't working properly," said Matriapoll. "It's supposed to be depositing the stuff here," he pointed to an orange area above the star's surface, "but it isn't doing that. It's putting it down *here*." He pointed to another area of the screen; the third planet.

"That's bad?"

Matriapoll turned to look at the two Mates. They sat on the back of his seat and looked back at him, tilting their heads to one side. Twoey licked his face.

"Don't you two *phnysthens* ever listen to the briefings?"

"Yes, of course we do."

"Then you ought to know that world's inhabited."

"Oh…it's *that* one. We thought it was the one with the pretty rings."

"Good grief," breathed Matriapoll, and took the scout-ship towards the offending planet.

The fighter rose above the airfield without a sound. The generals looked pleased. Cesare pretended not to be impressed. The plane was moving horizontally now, high enough for the people in the revue stand to be able to see the flat disk attached to its underside. It was that disk which was providing all the power. The craft swept away over the Nevada desert.

Somebody handed Cesare a pair of binoculars and told him where to watch. All he could see was a white blockhouse in the bright sun, shimmering, miles away.

Then the plane appeared in one corner of his magnified vision. A bolt of blinding light leapt from it, crossed to the blockhouse in no appreciable time, and demolished it in a cloud of dust.

"Hmm," Cesare said.

"What do you think, sir?" said the local I.M.C.C. head, a young man called Fosse.

"Depends. Can we produce those things?"

"We think we ought to be able to soon, sir. One of the last machines we recovered seems to like taking the others apart. We can start to find out exactly how they're put together. Once we find that out we're half-way there."

"OK, but where are these things coming from?"

"Frankly, sir, we don't know." They turned and looked back at the desert as the sound of the exploding blockhouse rolled over the stand. The aircraft was returning too, slowing for a vertical landing.

"We're sure they aren't Commie?"

"Oh, quite sure, sir. If they could deliver things that size into our air-space without our radar spotting them they'd be sending H-bombs, not their latest technology."

"Yes, that makes sense," Cesare said. The generals were

starting to file out of the stand. A fleet of helicopters waited for the various dignitaries, military and civilian. A handful of security men kept generals and other I.M.C.C. underlings from bothering Cesare as he chatted to Fosse.

"I understand the President has given us the full go-ahead for joint development with the armed forces, sir."

"Who? Oh, yeah. The President. Good. Real good. Get onto it then. I'm interested in this, Fosse. Think I'll stay over in California for a while. Get some rest. Keep an eye on all this. Pressure of work back in the East, you know."

"Of course, sir."

"Oh, shucks," Matriapoll said. "They've found them. Look at that." He showed them the writeout of all the objects the faulty Transporter had been beaming to Earth instead of the sun. The two little animals behind him went "tut-tut" and shook their heads. "Look at *that!*" Matriapoll went on, "A translator for the *Grenbrethg*, an automatic sewer inspection kit, a kiddie's climber, a *Bloorthana-ee* brothel hover-bed, a low-grade Repairer, a one-person gas sub, a *Striyian* phallic symbol, a... oh, no; a *Schpleebop* fly-swat!"

"Not so good, eh?" said Oney.

Matriapoll patted the hairy head of the little beast. "Correct, little one. Not good at all. A positive disaster; we could have a cargo-cult or anything down there by now. Warm up the ethergraph, I've got to get this back to the ship."

"... and however outlandish it may sound, it is my opinion that just as our great country has, in the past at least, seen fit to provide covert support for democracies under internal foreign subversion situations, so we ourselves are now being provided with aid by an alien super-power. And why is this? I'll tell you why. Because they recognize that the West, these United States of America, are the real representatives of humanity and decency on this planet. They want to help us to fend off the Communist threat. Now, whether we really need their help or not is a debatable moot point, it could be arguable...but if they want to give us this aid then I for one am not going to look a gift-horse in the mouth. I say we take this by the horns, and go for it."

Cesare sat down to restrained applause.

I.M.C.C.'s West Coast Headquarters Conference Room was packed with military and civilian personnel. They had all listened intently to what the scientists and generals had to say, and for many of them a lot of what they heard was new. The Company and the U.S.A.F., along with the Army and the Navy too, were launching a joint R&D programme on the New Technology (as they were calling it) and had every hope that they would soon have an unbeatable lead over the Soviets.

Personally, Cesare thought the Gifts were from God, but he'd been dissuaded from saying so, and the speech writers seemed to think Helpful Aliens was the most likely explanation. Cesare didn't think it mattered as long as they got the drop on the Commies.

"Great speech, sir," Fosse said afterwards.

"Thanks," Cesare said. "You're right. I think they all know what's going on now. But we have to watch the security angle on this real carefully now. Any leaks and the Ruskies might get windy and launch a pre-emptive."

"Well, I guess they'll find out eventually no matter how good our security is, sir. You know what some of the scientists are like."

"Hmm. And then they'll start a Third World War, the mad dogs."

"Yes. We'll just have to hope that we can develop the New Technology quickly enough so that—"

"Hmm."

Stardate: 0475 39709 G.M.T. (Galactic Mean Time). Ref: 283746352 = 728495 / dheyjquidhajvncjflzmxj / 27846539836574 / qwertyuiop + drmfsltd/MMM. Message begins: YOU STUPID HALF-ASSED INCOMPETENT MORONS YOU HAVE BEEN PUMPING THE

GOODS SLAP-BANG ONTO ONE OF THE MOST
RABIDLY SENSITIVE ROCK-BALLS IT HAS EVER
BEEN MY MISFORTUNE TO BE WITHIN A LIGHT-
YEAR OF. IF YOU COULD SEE THE MESS DOWN
HERE YOU WOULD VOMIT. I HAVE SEEN THE
MESS DOWN HERE AND I VOMITED ALL OVER
MY MATES AND THEY DID NOT LIKE IT. CLOSE
THAT (Expletive deleted by on-board ethergraph unit)
TRANSPORTER DOWN BEFORE THIS LOT BLOW
HALF THE PLANET AWAY. DISMANTLE THE
THING OR HACK IT TO BITS WITH AN AXE IF
YOU HAVE TO BUT *STOP IT*!

Yours sincerely,<br>7833 Matriapoll, C-U.S.3

Cesare was sitting in his Manhattan office with Fosse, who he had liked enough to bring through to the East Coast so that the younger man could see how things were run at the top.

"You finished with that yet?" Cesare said.

Fosse looked up from *It Pays to Increase Your Prayer Power.* "Yes, sir."

"Hmm." Cesare took the small magazine and slid a copy of a pamphlet called *God is a Businessman* across the desk to Fosse in exchange.

There was a knocking sound at the window.

The two men looked over in stunned surprise at a weird figure sitting on something that looked like a coffee table, floating in the air just outside the window. Whoever or what-ever it was, it was holding on to the coffee table with one hand, or paw, tapping the glass with another and with a third was playing absent-mindedly with the end of a bit of rope that was hanging in front of the window.

"Jeeeeeesus," Cesare gasped, reaching slowly for the drawer with the alarm on the outside and the Armalite on the inside.

The creature on the coffee table pushed lightly at the win-dow. It collapsed, and the being came inside, rubbing bits of glass off its furry spacesuit. Its face was a horrible bright red.

"First person singular obtaining colloquial orgasm within a Caledonian sandwich," it said, then looked annoyed, and spoke incoherently into a grille set in its belly, which replied. It looked up and said, "Sorry. As I was saying: I come in peace."

Cesare whipped out the Armalite and fired.

The bullets bounced off an invisible force-field, and one ricochetted back to Cesare's desk, totally destroying a very expensive executive toy. The creature on the coffee table looked upset.

"You bastard!" it yelled, and took a large pistol of its own from a holster and fired it at Cesare. A cloud of green glowing gas enveloped Cesare's face, which dropped. He let the gun drop too.

"My God," he breathed, "I've crapped my pants." He stumbled waddling away from the desk and into his private toilet, doubled up and holding the seat of his trousers.

The creature was looking into the muzzle of his pistol and scratching its head with one foot. "That's funny," it said, "it's meant to make your eyes explode."

It floated over to Fosse, stopping at the desk to lick appreciatively at the blue glop that had flowed, slowly, from the smashed executive toy.

Fosse, sweating, smiled ingratiatingly and said, "I think we're going to get along just fine..."

The MPs came for the other Air Force general. He'd been away so long it had been assumed he'd deserted. They dragged him out kicking and screaming.

The professor watched phlegmatically. Ever since the foreign minister had been informed that there'd been a coup back home and he would be placed under house arrest at the embassy if he left, the professor had resigned himself to whatever happened here. He'd even let the general who had just been arrested make models of the planned bomber from the papers of the Alternative Resources Project.

He didn't know why he bothered staying, but what the hell...

"...so you see when you're producing so much material from a factory ship that size you have to maximize the optimum output both in terms of real numbers and as a viable proportion of total units produced. With the high rates of production attainable using light atoms and dust to build up or break down to basic molecules which then go to construct artefacts, naturally you have a certain proportion that fail to meet the quite perfect standards we set.

"All such material is dumped onto the surface of a nearby star or, in the case of high heat-resistance articles, dumped somewhere inside it. The material cannot be recycled economically because as a rule even the shoddy goods that we produce are very difficult to break up, and the Transmuters are tuned only to accept matter in comparatively small quanta. In this case there seems to have been rather a serious leak. The new machinery we've just installed has made a mistake in the relevant coordinates, and...well, you know the rest."

"You mean all this stuff is RUBBISH?" said Cesare from the bathroom.

"Yes, I'm afraid so. There shouldn't be any more after a little while. I've already contacted the factory ship. Please accept our sincere apologies."

"Wait a minute," Fosse said as the alien turned to go. "Have these things been arriving just *anywhere*? I mean is it a random thing?"

"Yes. The Transporter got that right, at least. They've been distributed fairly evenly over the globe. Most of them have sunk in the oceans of course, and quite a few are still undiscovered in rainforests and deserts and in the Antarctic and so on, but we'll locate those through their coverings and get rid of them once we get another new machine on-line." It held up three paws as Fosse started to speak again. "I know," it said, "you'd like to keep the things, but I'm afraid that isn't possible.

We do have a responsibility, after all. Now you must excuse me. Goodbye."

The alien disappeared out of the window and went straight up into the sky, narrowly missing a passing S.S.T.

Suddenly the alarm started sounding. Five armed guards rushed into the room and began restraining Fosse. Cesare succeeded in stopping them before Fosse had anything worse than severe bruising and a broken jaw. He shooed the guards out and closed the door.

"You realize what this means?" he said to Fosse. "I'll tell you what it means; we're using *junk*; that's what it means!"

"It'sh worsh than that, shir," Fosse said. "That shing shaid the Gi—rubbish wash appearing all over the surfashe of the Earth; that meansh the bigg—ow!—the bi'er the country the more of thoshe thingsh they're going to get; and rubbish or not they can probably all be ushed."

"So?"

"Do you know what country hash the greatesht landarea in the whole world, shir?"

Cesare nodded confidently. "The good old U.S. of A."

"No, shir," Fosse said shaking his head slowly.

Cesare looked into Fosse's eyes. His own eyes gradually widened and his upper lip trembled. "Not..."

"Yesh!"

"Hot-damn!"


The Gifts kept appearing for two more weeks, which they guessed was the time it took for the Alien's message to get to the factory ship, and/or the time it took for the rubbish to get from the ship to Earth.

They kept testing the equipment but if there was anything wrong with it they couldn't find out what it was. The aliens must be really fussy.

The very last Gift to arrive, as far as they knew, was the most interesting of all. The New Technology Project was racing ahead, budget vastly increased now that it was known the

Communists probably had the same stuff. The spy satellites hadn't spotted anything, but then they'd managed to keep pretty tight security themselves, so that didn't prove anything.

They were near Alamogordo, where the last, very large Gift had appeared. They had had to construct a special building around it to do the business with the covering. Cesare looked up at it.

"OK. But what does it do?"

"It's a matter transmission machine," said one scientist.

"No, it isn't," said another. "Whatever it is it isn't that; it doesn't leave an original behind. I think it uses continua to—"

"Rubbish. It's a true matter transmission machine, Mr. Borges. We can't hope to recreate this with our own technology, but we can certainly use it; shifting commodities, urgently needed drugs, disaster aid..."

"There's nothing wrong with it?"

"Wrong with it? Why, this is the most perfect piece of machinery in existence on the planet. We've already shifted two hundred *brand-new* Cadillacs from here to Tampa and back again just as a trial. It did it without a murmur and right on target."

"Good."

"Now, as I was saying...we could use this thing to vastly step up the productive capacity of certain key industries, and make possible the rapid deployment of emergency supplies in a disaster/crisis situation—"

*Good*, thought Cesare. *We can use it to bomb the Ruskies.*

"What?" roared Matriapoll when he got back and they told him. "You told it to junk itself and it disappeared up its *own* asshole!"

"It was an honest mistake," said Matriapoll's foreman.

"They'll use it! They'll infest every nearby planet and system they can lay their coordinates on!"

"It'll probably malfunction totally sooner or later; don't worry about it. By the way, where's your other Mate? I only see one."

"Don't talk to me about it," Matriapoll said huffily. "The idiot took a Flyer for a joy-ride and collided with an S.S.T."

"You're sure this is going to work sir?"

"Sure it'll work," Cesare said. They were sitting with a whole load of I.M.C.C. people and military and political types in the underground command-post under the matter transmitter. "We tested it by sending the same number of dummy warheads right round the world and back here. They were all bang-on. It'll be a clean sweep. Nothing can go wrong."

The Transporter, unduly sensitive to, amongst other things, radiation, became somewhat mixed up however, and, to cut a short story shorter, it blitzed the Eastern seaboard of the United States of America, messed the Atlantic up a bit, and bombed Mauritania, Portugal and Ireland. After that it jammed and never worked again.

Fosse thought that Mr. Borges was taking it very well, considering (there was talk of a law suit). Cesare was on the phone, trying to trace somebody.

"Anybody I know, sir?"

Cesare looked up from the telephone, his eyes reflecting the embarrassing red splotches spread over the giant world map on the far side of the room. "You remember Feldman? Professor Feldman?"

"No, sir; I don't think I've ever met the person."

"Doesn't matter; he's dead. But I'm getting hold of his number two in Chicago; he's all right. I've heard what it's like in the East. It sounds terrible: famine, plague, cannibalism, anarchy, flooding, drought; the works. There's fantastic scope for a pet project of mine I've been nursing along for a few years now. Called the Alternative Resources Project. It's perfect for this situation. We're ideally placed to take advantage of this. It's a peach, believe me. We could clean up."

# Piece

H i kid. Well, there I was about to do some reading but instead I'm writing to you. I'll explain later, but first a little story (bear with me—this is partly to take my mind off things, including the book I was starting to read, but also to set up the first of a couple of coincidences. Anyway.)

It was...1975, I think; have to check my diaries to be sure. I'd finished at Uni that spring and gone off hitchhiking through Europe over the summer. Paris, Bergen, Berlin, Venice, Rabat and Madrid defined the limits of this whirlwind tour. Three months later I was on my way home, and after staying with Aunt Jess in Crawley, I'd used the last of my money to buy a bus ticket from London to Glasgow (hitching out of London was notoriously awful). Night bus, and it took ages, staying off the motorways would you believe. This was in the days before videos and minibars and hostesses and even toilets on buses. The old coach groaned and whined through the rain-smeared darkness, stopping at breeze block and Formica transport cafes; cold islands of fluorescence in the night.

Especially then, buses were for the not so well off. I was the scruffy hitcher with long hair and jeans. I was sitting beside an old guy wearing shiny trousers and a worn tweed jacket; thin limbs and thick glasses. In front of us, an old lady reading *People's Friend*; behind, two lads with yesterday's *Sun*. The usual girning baby and harassed young mother, somewhere at the back. I watched the sodium lights drift by in droplet lines of orange, and alternated sitting upright in the cramped seat, and sliding down into it, aching knees against the back of the seat in front. And, for the first couple of hours or so, I was reading some SF novel (wish I could remember the name, but can't).

Later I tried sleeping. It wasn't easy; you swung fretfully in and out, never fully awake or completely asleep, always conscious of the growling gear changes and the creaky ache in folded knees. Then the old guy started talking to me.

I'm one of these anti-social types—well, as you know—who doesn't like to acknowledge the presence of other people when I'm travelling; plus I was quite shy back then (believe it or not), and I really didn't want to talk to some old geezer I imagined I had nothing in common with. But he started the conversation and I couldn't be rude and just cut it off. If I remember right, he pointed at the SF book, wedged between my leg and the arm rest.

"You believe in all that stuff then, do you?" Scottish accent, not strong, maybe Borders or Edinburgh.

I sighed. Here we go, I thought. "Sorry? How do you mean?"

"UFOs and all that"

"Well, no." I riffled the pages of the paperback, as though looking for clues. "I just like science fiction. Not much of it's about UFOs; this isn't. I probably wouldn't read one about UFOs."

"Oh." He looked at the book (I was getting embarrassed by its gaudy, irrelevant cover, and put it away). "Are you a student?"

"Yes. Well, no; I was. I graduated."

"Ah. Science, was it, you were doing?"

"English."

"Oh. But you like science?"

I'm sure that's the way he put it. I jotted a lot of this down next day, and wrote a poem about it—"Jack"—a couple of months later, and I'm sure if I had my notes with me they'd confirm that was how he put it: "You *like* science?"

So we got on to what he'd always wanted to talk about.

He—yes, his name was Jack—couldn't understand how people thought they could tell something was so many million years old. How could anyone tell what came when and where? He couldn't understand; he was a Christian and the Bible seemed much more sensible.

Ever felt your heart sink? We'd been on the road two hours, we were barely past Northampton, and I was stuck—probably for the whole of the rest of the journey, judging from the guy's accent—beside some ancient geek who thought the universe was created about tea-time in 4004 BC. Holy shit.

Being young and stupid, I did actually try to explain (I watched "Horizon"; I got *New Scientist*, sometimes).

Let the poem take up the story (from memory, so make allowances):

And Christ, dear reader, what could I do?
    Oh, I made the lame, half-hearted try;
    I told him all was linked, that those same laws
    Of physics, chemistry, and math that let him sit here,
    In this bus, with the engine, on that road,
    Dictated through the ages what was so.
    Carbon 14 I mentioned, its slow and sure decay,
    Even magnetic alignments, frozen in the rocks
    By the heat of ancient fires;
    The associated fossils, floating continents,
    Erosion, continuity and change…
    But from the first tired syllable, in fact before,
    I knew it was pointless.
    And somewhere back
    Of all that well-informed-layman stuff,
    Something a little more like the real me listened,
    And looked at the old man's glasses.
    —They were old, with thick frames, dark brown.
    The glass too was thick, and thick with dust.
    Dandruff, dead scales of old flesh, hairs
    Cemented there by grease and stale sweat,
    Obscured the views the scratches didn't.
    And even if the prescription wasn't years ago exceeded
    By his dying sight,
    The grime; that personal, impersonal dust,
    Sapped the bulky lenses of their use

And, removed, inspected,
How could those rheumy eyes unaided see
This aggravation of their disability?

(This was when I was into using rhyme only very sparingly,
like any other poetic effect.) There was more, rather labouring
the point about "views" and cloudy thinking and so on, but
passing swiftly on, we come to:

He took in nothing.
    My throat got sore.
    The Borders came, and soon he left, met by his sister
    In some dismal little rain-soaked town.

OK? So Cut To:

Last week. Me with the hard core of the Creative Writing Group
on an Intercity 125, heading for London for a reading at the
ICA (Kathy Acker, Martin Millar, etc). I was sitting across
from Mo—the good-looking Indian guy with the tash; very
bright; chose us instead of Oxbridge, God knows why—and
I tipped my micro-bottle of Grouse into the plastic glass and
took out the book I was going to start reading, and Mo…
just tensed. I'm not too hot on body language; I miss a lot, I
know (you see—I do listen to what you say), but it was like
Mo suddenly became an ice statue, and these waves of cold
antagonism started flowing across the table at me. The others
noticed too, and went quiet.

So I'd taken *The Satanic Verses* by Salman Rushdie out of the
old daypack, hadn't I? And Mo's sitting there like he expects
the book to bubble and squirm and burst into flames right
there in my hands.

Now, I don't know how much you've heard about the ker-
fuffle surrounding this book—it hasn't exactly been front
page news, and with any luck it won't be—but since it was
published quite a few Muslims have been demanding it be

banned, withdrawn or whatever because it contains—so they say—some sort of semi-blasphemous material in it relating to the Koran. I'd talked about this general area of authorial freedom and religious censorship with a couple of classes, but still hadn't read the novel, and it just hadn't occurred to me somebody like Mo—who hadn't been in either of those classes—might be on the side of the bad guys.

"Mo; is there a problem?"

"That is not a good book, Mr. Munro," he said, looking at it, not me. "It is evil; blasphemous." (Embarrassed silence from the others.)

"Look, Mo, I'll put the book away if it offends you," I told him (doing just that). "But I think we have to talk about this. All right; I haven't read the book myself yet, but I was talking to Doctor Metcalf the other day, and he said he had, and the passages some people found objectionable were...a couple of pages at most, and he couldn't see what the fuss was about. I mean, this is a novel, Mo. It isn't a...religious tract; it *means* to be fiction."

"That isn't the point, Mr. Munro," Mo said. He was looking at my little red rucksack as though there was a nuclear bomb inside it. "Rushdie has insulted all Muslims. He has spat in the face of every one of us. It's as if he has called all our mothers whores."

"Mo," I said, and couldn't help grinning as I put the rucksack down on the floor, "it's only a story."

"The form is not important. It is a work in which Allah is insulted," Mo said. "You can't understand, Mr. Munro. There is nothing you hold that sacred."

"Oh no? How about freedom of speech?"

"But when the National Front wanted to use the Students' Union, you were with us on the demonstration, weren't you? What about their freedom of speech?"

"They want to take it away from everybody else; come on, Mo. You're not denying them freedom of speech, you're protecting the freedoms of the people they'd persecute if they were allowed any power."

"But in the short term you *are* denying them the right to state their views in public, are you not?"

"The way you'd deny somebody the freedom to put a gun to another person's head and pull the trigger, yes."

"So, clearly your belief in freedom generally can override any particular freedom; these freedoms are not absolute. Nothing is sacred to you, Mr. Munro. You base your beliefs on the products of human thought, so it could hardly be otherwise. You might believe in certain things, but you do not have *faith.* That comes with submission to the force of divine revelation."

"So because I don't have what I think of as superstitions, because I believe we just happen to exist, and believe in... science, evolution, whatever; I'm not as...worthy as somebody who has faith in an ancient book and a cruel, desert God? I'm sorry, Mo, but for me, Christ and Muhammed were both just men; charismatic, gifted in various ways, but still just mortal human beings, and the scholars and monks and disciples and historians who wrote about them or recorded their thoughts and their lives were inspired all right, but not by God; by something from inside them, something every writer has... in fact something every human has. Mo; definitions. Faith is belief without proof. I can't accept that. Now, it doesn't bother me that you can, so why does it bother you so much that I think the way I do, or Salman Rushdie thinks the way he does?"

"Clearly, your soul is your own concern, Mr. Munro. Rushdie's is his. To think blasphemous thoughts is to restrict the sin to oneself, but to blaspheme in public is deliberately to assault those who do believe. It is to rape our souls."

Can you believe this? This guy's heading for a First; his father's an astro-physicist, for Christ's sake. Mo's probably going to be a lecturer himself (he already puts "clearly" at the start of his sentences; good grief, he's halfway there!). It's very nearly 1989 but it's midnight in the dark ages just the thickness of a book away, the thickness of a skull away; just the turn of a page away.

So, an argument, while the leafless trees and the cold brown fields stream by beyond the carriage's double-glazing, and the inevitable wailing child howled somewhere in the distance.

But what do you say? I asked him about the kids who rode across the minefields on their Hondas, clearing the way for the Iranian Army, the hard way. Insane, to me. To Mo? Maybe misguided, maybe used, but still glorious. I told him that while I hadn't read *The Satanic Verses*, I had read the Koran, and found it almost as ludicrous and objectionable as the Bible... and after that I got a bit loud, while Mo went very quiet and forbidding and curt, and one of the others had verbally to separate us. (Coincidence; I read the Penguin edition of the Koran—edited by a Jew, Mo claims, and unholy too because it puts the passages in the wrong order—and Viking, who publish "TSV," are part of the same group...fertile ground for a conspiracy theory?)

Mo and I shook hands, later on, but it spoiled the day.

Good place to pause. They've just called us.

Hi again. Well, here I am, Bloody Mary in one hand, pen in the other, using Rushdie's book to lean on. Got an aisle to one side, empty seat to the other, so I can spread myself out (already taken my shoes off). Bit less crowded than I'd expected at this time of year. Jacksonville here I come. (I guess if it had been Harvard they'd have paid for Clipper Class, but you can't have everything.)

Right. The coincidences I was talking about. I started reading *The Satanic Verses* in the departure lounge there, and how does it begin? With two guys falling through the air after being blown up in a jumbo jet. Great. I mean not that I'm a nervous flier or anything, but this is not what one wishes to read before boarding a plane, correct? So that's one. Plus those other two instances; of travel, a conversation/argument started by a book (by two books), reason against faith both times, somehow seem to belong together with this journey;

bus, train, plane, a travelling trinity of functioning technology to compare and contrast with the paranoid psychoses of religious belief.

What do you do with these people? (Never mind what they might do to us, if they ever get the whip hand; what chance would I have to teach "Reason and Compassion in Twentieth-Century Poetry" in Tehran?) Reason shapes the future, but superstition infects the present.

And coincidence convinces the credulous. Two things happen at the same time, or one after another, and we assume there must be a link; well, we sacrificed a virgin last year, and there *was* a good harvest. Of course the ceremony to raise the sun works—it comes up every morning doesn't it? I say my prayers each night and the world hasn't ended yet…

Dung beetle thinking. Life is too complicated for there not to be continual coincidences, and we just have to come to terms with the fact that they merely happen and aren't ordained, that some things occur for no real reason whatsoever, and that this is not a punishment and that is not a reward. Good grief; the most copper-bottomed, platinum-card proof of divine intervention, of some holy master-plan, would be if there were no coincidences at all! That really *would* look suspicious.

I don't know. Maybe I'm the one who's wrong. I don't mean that either the Christians or the Muslims actually have the truth, that either the geriatric gibberings of Rome or the hysterical spurtings out of Qom contain anything remotely resembling the real bottom line about Where We Come From or What It's All About, but that both might represent the way humanity truly wants to be; perhaps they are its truest images. Maybe reason is the aberration (thought perishes).

A little girl—long curly blonde hair, enormous blue eyes, with one of those unspillable plastic cups held chubbily in both hands—has just appeared in the aisle beside me, expression very serious. She's gazing at me with that disinterested intensity only little kids seem to be capable of. Gone again.

Absolutely gorgeous. But how do I know her parents aren't

Christian fundamentalists and she won't grow up sincerely believing Darwin was an agent of the devil and evolution a dangerous nonsense?

I guess I don't. (Hey! I used "guess" instead of "suppose"! I'm thinking like an American already!) I guess I don't, and it wouldn't matter if I did. Let the crazies burn rock albums and hunt the Ark on Ararat; *let* them look stupid while we look to the future. We just have to hope there are always more of us than there are of them, or at least that we are more influential, better placed. Whatever.

Whatever indeed. I smell food. My semi-circular canals tell me—I think—that we are starting to level out, reaching our cruising altitude. Dark outside the windows. Last coincidence:

I never did specify in the poem, but the wee daft town—dismal, rain-soaked—in "Jack" was called Lockerbie (about the only time you might have seen or heard the name was when we were driving up to Scotland—it's just off the A74, not far over the border). And—according to this handy route map in my very own complimentary Pan Am in-flight mag—we'll fly right over it. I suspect old Jack kicked the bucket years ago, to go to whatever award he imagined might be his, but if he isn't dead, and he does look out of his window tonight (and he finally cleaned his glasses), I wonder if he

(Piece PP/n.k.no. 29271, recovered grid ref. NY 241 770, at 1435 on 24/12/88. A4 Refill Pad, part, torn.)

# The State of the Art

## CONTENTS

# The State of the Art

## 1: Excuses And Accusations

| | |
|---|---:|
| Parharengyisa | Rasd-Codurersa |
| Listach | Diziet |
| Ja'andeesih | Embless |
| Petrain | Sma |
| dam Kotosklo | da'Marenhide |
| (location as name) | (c/o SC) |
| | 2.288-93 |

Dear Mr. Petrain

I do hope you will accept my apologies for keeping you waiting so long. Included herewith—at last!—is the information you asked me for all that time ago. My personal well-being, after which you so kindly enquired, is all I could hope for. As you will probably have been told, and doubtless observed from my location (or rather lack of it) above, I am no longer in Contact *ordinaire*, and my position in Special Circumstances is such that I occasionally have to leave my present address for considerable periods of time, often with only a few hours notice during which to attend personally to any outstanding business. Apart from these sporadic jaunts, my life is one of lazy luxury on a sophisticated stage three-four (uncontacted) where I enjoy all the benefits of an interestingly, if not exotically, foreign planet sufficiently developed to possess a reasonably civilized demeanour without suffering overmuch the global sameness which so often accompanies such progress.

A pleasant life, then, and when I am called away it usually feels more like a holiday than an unwelcome interruption. In fact, the only grit in the eye is a rather self-important Offensive-model drone whose exaggerated concern for my physical safety, if not my peace of mind, frequently becomes more exasperating than it is comforting (my theory is that SC finds drones whose robust pugnacity has led them to some overly-violent act in the past and then tells these pathological devices to guard their human Special Circumstancer successfully, or be componented. But that is by the bye).

Anyway, what with the remoteness of my habitation and the fact I've been off-planet for the past hundred days or so (with drone, of course), and the delay while I consulted my notes and tried to dig from my memory what scraps of conversation and "atmosphere" I could, and then fretting over the best way to present the resulting data... well, all this has taken rather a long time, and to be honest the sedate mode of my present life has not helped me to be as brisk as I would have liked in the execution of this task.

I am glad to hear that you are only one of many scholars specializing in Earth; I always did think the place well worth studying, and perhaps even learning from. Thankfully, then, you will have all the information that could possibly qualify as background, and I apologize in advance if anything I include doubles on this; but while I have stuck as strictly as memory (machine and human) will allow to what actually happened those hundred and fifteen years ago, I have nevertheless tried to make the presentation of the following events and impressions as general and self-contained as possible, believing this to be the best way of attempting to conform with your request to describe what it really felt like to be there at the time. I trust this combination of fact and sensation does not unduly affect the utility of either when you come to process the result in the course of your studies, but in the event that it does, and also if you have any other questions about Earth at that time which you think I might be able to help answer, please do not hesitate to get in touch with me; I am only too happy to shed what light I can on a place that affected everyone who was there both profoundly and—in the main, I suspect—permanently.

What follows, then, is as much as I and my bank can remember. The conversations I have had to reconstruct, as a rule; I did not then practise full-record, it being a minor piece of the ship's (frankly tediously) eccentric etiquette not to "over-observe" (its words) life on board. Some dialogue, mostly on-planet, was recorded, however, and I have placed these sections between the following two symbols: ‹ ›. They have undergone a degree of tidying up—removing the usual "umms" and "ahs" and so on—but the original recordings are available to you from my bank without further authorization, should you feel you require them. For the sake of brevity I have reduced all Full Names to one or two parts, and done my best to anglicize them. All the times and dates are Earth-relative/local (Christian calendar).

Incidentally, I was most pleased to receive your news about the *Arbitrary* and its escapades over these last few decades; I confess to having been rather out of touch recently, and became quite nostalgic on hearing again of that misfit machine.

But back to Earth, and back all those years ago, and by the way my English has suffered over the past century of neglect; the drone is translating all this, and any mistakes are bound to be its.

Diziet Sma

## 2: Stranger Here Myself

### 2.1: *Well I Was In The Neighbourhood*

By the spring of the year 1977 AD, the General Contact Unit *Arbitrary* had been stationed above the planet Earth for the best part of six months. The ship, of the Escarpment class, middle series, had arrived during the previous November after clipping the edge of the planet's expanding electro-magnetic emission shell while on what it claimed was a random search. How random the search pattern was I don't know; the ship might well have had some information it wasn't telling us about, some scrap of rumour half remembered from somebody's long-discredited archives, multitudinously translated and re-transmitted, vague and uncertain after all that time and movement and change; just a mention that there was an intelligent human-ish species there, or at least the beginnings of one, or the possibility of one... You could ask the ship itself about this easily enough, but getting an answer might be another matter (you know what GCUs are like).

Anyway, there we were over an almost classic sophisticated stage three perfect enough to have come right out of the book, from a footnote if not a main chapter. I think everybody, including the ship, was delighted. We all knew the chances of stumbling across something like Earth were remote, even looking in the most likely places (which we weren't, officially), yet all we had to do was switch on the nearest screen or our own terminals and see it hanging there, in real space, less than a microsecond away, shining blue and white (or black velvet scattered with light motes), its wide, innocent face ever changing. I remember staring at it for hours at a time on occasion, watching the weather patterns' slow swirl if we were stationary relative to it, or gazing at its rolling curve of water, cloud and land mass if we were moving. It looked at once serene and warm, implacable and vulnerable. The contradictory nature of these impressions worried me for reasons I could not fully articulate, and contributed to a vague feeling of apprehension I already had that somehow the place was a little too close to some perfection, slightly too textbookish for its own good.

It needed thinking about, of course. Even while the *Arbitrary* was still turning and decelerating, and then running through the old radio waves on its way to their source, it was both pondering itself and signalling the General Systems Vehicle *Bad For Business*, which was tramping a thousand years core-ward, and which we had left after a rest and refit only a year before. What else the *Bad* might have contacted to help it mull over the problem is probably on record somewhere, but I haven't considered it important enough to search out. While the *Arbitrary* described graceful power-orbits around Earth and the great Minds were considering whether to contact or not, most of us in the *Arbitrary* were in a frenzy of preparation.

For the first few months of its stay the ship acted like a gigantic sponge, soaking up every scrap, every bit of information it could find anywhere on the planet, scouring tape and card and file and disc and fiche and film and tablet and page and scroll, recording and filming and photographing, measuring and charting and mapping, sorting and collating and analyzing.

A fraction of this avalanche of data (it felt like a lot but it was actually pifflingly small, the ship assured us) was stuffed into the heads of those of us sufficiently close in physique to pass for human on Earth, after a little alteration (I got a couple of extra toes, a joint removed from each finger and a rather generalized ear, nose and cheekbone job. The ship insisted on teaching me to walk differently as well), and so by the start of '77 I was fluent in German and English and probably knew more about the history and current affairs of the place than the vast majority of its inhabitants.

I knew Dervley Linter moderately well, but then one knows everybody on a ship of only three hundred people. He had been on the *Bad for Business* at the same time as I, but we had only met after we both joined the *Arbitrary*. Both of us had been in Contact for about half the standard stretch, so neither of us were exactly novices. This, to me, makes his subsequent course of action doubly mystifying.

I was based in London for January and February, spending the time tramping through museums (viewing exhibits the ship already had perfect 4D holos of, and not seeing the crated artefacts there wasn't room to show which were stored in basements or somewhere else entirely, which the ship *also* had perfect holos of), going to movies (which the ship of course had copies of compiled from the very best prints), and—more relevantly, perhaps—attending concerts, plays, sports events and every sort and type of gathering and meeting the ship could discover. I spent quite a lot of time just walking around and looking, getting people talking. All very dutiful, but not always as easy or stress-free as it sounds; the bizarre sexual *mores* of the locals could make it surprisingly awkward for a woman simply to go up and start talking to a man. I suspect if I hadn't been a good ten centimetres taller than the average male I'd have had more trouble than I did.

My other problem was the ship itself. It was always trying to get me to visit as many places as possible, do as much as I could, see all the people I was able to; look at this, listen to that, meet her, talk to him, watch that, wear this...it wasn't so much that we wanted to do different things— the ship rarely tried to get me to do anything I wouldn't want to do—simply that the thing wanted me to be doing something *all the time.* I was its envoy to the city, its one human tendril, a root through which it sucked with all its might, trying to feed the apparently bottomless pit it called its memory.

I took holidays from the rush, in the remote, wild places; Ireland's Atlantic coast and the Scottish highlands and islands. In County Kerry, in Galway and Mayo, in Wester Ross and Sutherland and Mull and Lewis I dallied while the ship tried to bring me back with threats and cajolings and promises of all the exciting work it had for me to do.

But in early March I was finished in London, so I was sent to Germany and told to wander, asked to drift and travel round and given a few places and dates, things to do and see and think about.

Now that I had stopped *using* English, as it were, I felt free to start reading works in that language for pleasure, and that was what I did in my spare time, what little of it there was.

The year turned, gradually there was less snow, the air became warmer, and after thousands upon thousands of kilometres of roads and railway tracks and dozens of hotel rooms, I was called back in late April to the ship, to reel off my thoughts and feelings to it. The ship was trying hard to get the mood of the planet, to form the sort of impression that only direct human interaction can provide the raw material for. It was sorting and rearranging and randomizing and re-sorting its data, looking for patterns and themes, and trying to gauge and relate all the sensations its human agents had encountered, measuring them against whatever conclusions of its own it had come to while swimming through the ocean of facts and figures it had already dredged from the world. We were by no means finished, of course, and I and all the others who were down on-planet would be there for some months yet, but it was time to get some first impressions.

*2.2: A Ship With A View*

"So you think we should contact, do you?"

I was lying, sleepy and contented and full after a large dinner,
sprawled over a cushion couch in a rec area with the lights
dimmed, my feet on the arm of the seat, my arms folded,
my eyes closed. A gentle, warm draught, vaguely Alpine in
its fragrance, was displacing the smell of the food I and
some of my friends had consumed. They were off playing
some game in another part of the ship, and I could just hear
their voices over the Bach I had persuaded the ship to like,
and which it was now playing for me.

"Yes I do. And as soon as possible, too."

"They'd be upset."

"Too bad. It's for their own good." I opened my eyes and
flashed what was, I hoped, a palpably contrived smile at
the ship's remote drone, which was sitting at a slightly
drunken angle on the arm of the couch. Then I closed my
eyes again.

"Probably it would be, but that isn't the point, really."

"What is the point then, really?" I knew the answer too well
already, but kept hoping the ship would come up with a
more convincing reason than the one I knew it was going
to give. Maybe one day.

"How," the ship said through the drone, "can we be sure
we're doing the right thing? How do we know what is—or
would be—for their own good, unless, over a very long
period, we observe matched areas of interest—in this case
planets—and compare the effects of contacting and not
contacting?"

"We ought to know well enough by now. Why sacrifice this
place to some experiment we already know the results of?"

"Why sacrifice it to your own restless conscience?"

I opened one eye and looked at the remote drone on the
couch arm. "A moment ago we agreed it would probably
be for the best, for them, if we went in. Don't try and cloud

the issue. We could do it, we should do it. That's what I think."

"Yes," said the ship, "but even so there would be technical difficulties, given the volatility of the situation. They're on a cusp; a highly heterogeneous but highly connected—and stressedly connected—civilization. I'm not sure that one approach could encompass the needs of their different systems. The particular stage of communication they're at, combining rapidity and selectivity, usually with something added to the signal and almost always with something missed out, means that what passes for truth often has to travel at the speed of failing memories, changing attitudes and new generations. Even when this form of handicap is recognized all they ever try to do, as a rule, is codify it, manipulate it, tidy it up. Their attempts to filter become part of the noise, and they seem unable to bring any more thought to bear on the matter than that which leads them to try and simplify what can only be understood by coming to terms with its complexity."

"Uh…right," I said, still trying to work out exactly what the ship was talking about.

"Hmm," the ship said.

When the ship says "Hmm," it's stalling. The beast takes no appreciable time to think, and if it pretends it does then it must be waiting for you to say something to it. I out-foxed it though; I said nothing.

But, looking back at what we were talking about, and what we each said we thought, and trying to imagine what it was really about, I do believe that it was then it decided to use me as it did. That "Hmm" marked a decision that meant I was involved the way I was in the Linter affair, and that was what the ship was really worried about; that which, all evening, during the meal and afterwards, slipping in the odd remark, the occasional question, the ship was really asking me about. But I didn't know that at the time. I was just sleepy and full and contented and warm and lying there talking to thin air, while the remote drone sat on the arm of the couch and talked to me.

"Yes," sighed the ship at last, "for all our data and sophistication and analyses and statistically correct generalizations, these things remain singular and uncertain."

"Aw," I tutted, "it's a hard life being a GCU. Poor ship, poor Papageno."

"You may mock, my little chick," the ship said with a sort of fakedly hurt sniffiness, "but the final responsibility remains mine."

"Ah, you're an old fraud, machine." I grinned over at the drone. "You'll get no sympathy out of me. You know what I think; I've told you."

"You don't think we'd spoil the place? You seriously think they're ready for us? For what we'd do to them even with the best of intentions?"

"*Ready* for it? What does that matter? What does it even *mean*? Of course they aren't ready for it, of course we'll spoil the place. Are they any more ready for World War Three? You seriously think we could mess the place up more than they're doing at the moment? When they're not actually out slaughtering each other they're inventing ingenious new ways to massacre each other more efficiently in the future, and when they're not doing *that* they're committing speciescide, from the Amazon to Borneo . . . or filling the seas with shit, or the air, or the land. They could hardly make a better job of vandalizing their own planet if we gave them lessons."

"But you still like them, I mean as people, the way they are."

"No, *you* like them the way they are," I told the ship, pointing at the remote drone. "They appeal to your sense of untidiness. You think I haven't been listening all the times you've gone on about how we're 'infecting the whole galaxy with sterility' . . . isn't that the phrase?"

"I may have used that form of words," the ship agreed vaguely, "but don't you think—"

"Oh, I can't be bothered thinking now," I said, levering myself off the couch. I stood up, yawning and stretching. "Where's the gang gone?"

"Your companions are about to watch an amusing film I found on-planet."

"Fine," I said. "I'll watch it too. Which way?"

The remote drone floated up from the couch arm. "Follow me." I left the alcove where we'd eaten. The drone turned round as it meandered through curtains and around chairs, tables and plants. It looked back at me. "You don't want to talk to me? I only want to explain—"

"Tell you what, ship. You wait here and I'll hit dirt and find you a priest and you can unburden yourself to him. The *Arbitrary* goes to confession. Definitely an idea whose time has come." I waved at some people I hadn't seen for a while, and kicked some cushions out of my way. "You could tidy this place up a bit, too."

"Your wish..." the remote drone sighed and stopped to supervise the cushions, which were dutifully re-arranging themselves. I stepped down into a darkened, sound-shrouded area where people were sitting or lying in front of a 2D screen. The film was just starting. It was science fiction, of all things; called *Dark Star*. Just before I stepped through the soundfield I heard the remote drone behind me sigh to itself again. "Ah, it's true what they say; April is the cruellest month..."


*2.3: Unwitting Accomplice*

It was about a week later, when I was due to go back on-planet, to Berlin, when the ship wanted to talk to me again. Things were going on as usual; the *Arbitrary* spent its time making detailed maps of everything within sight and without, dodging American and Soviet satellites and manufacturing and then sending down to the planet hundreds upon thousands of bugs to watch printing works and magazine stalls and libraries, to scan museums, workshops, studios and shops, to look into windows, gardens and forests, and to track buses, trains, cars, seaships and planes. Meanwhile its effectors, and those on its main satellites, probed every computer, monitored every landline, tapped every microwave link, and listened to every radio transmission on Earth.

All Contact craft are natural raiders. They're made to love to be busy, to enjoy sticking their big noses into other people's business, and the *Arbitrary*, for all its eccentricities, was no different. I doubt if it was, or is, ever happier than when doing that vacuum-cleaner act above a sophisticated planet. By the time we were ready to leave the ship would have contained in its memory—and would have onward-transmitted to other vessels—every bit of data ever stored in the history of the planet that hadn't been subsequently obliterated. Every 1 and 0, every letter, every pixel, every sound, every subtlety of line and texture ever fashioned. It would know where every mineral deposit was buried, where all the treasure as yet undiscovered lay, where every sunken ship was, where every secret grave had been dug; and it would know the secrets of the Pentagon, the Kremlin, the Vatican...

On Earth, of course, they were quite oblivious to the fact they had a million tonnes of highly inquisitive and outrageously powerful alien spaceship orbiting around them, and—sure enough—the locals were doing all the things *they* normally did; murdering and starving and dying and maiming and torturing and lying and so on. Pretty much business as usual in fact, and it bothered the hell out of me, but I was still hoping we'd decide to interfere and stop most of that shit. It was about this time two Boeing 747s collided on the ground in a Spanish island colony.

I was reading *Lear* for the second time, sitting underneath a full-size palm tree. The ship had found the tree in the

Dominican Republic, marked to be bulldozed to make way
for a new hotel. Thinking it might be nice to have some
plants about the place, the *Arbitrary* dug the palm up one
night and brought it aboard, complete with its root system
and several tens of cubic metres of sandy soil, and planted it
in the centre of our accommodation section. This required
quite a lot of rearranging, and a few people who'd happened to be asleep while all this was going on woke to
be confronted with a twenty-metre high tree when they
opened their cabin doors, rising up in what had become
a great central well in the acc section. Contact people are
used to putting up with this sort of thing from their ships,
however, and so everybody took it in their stride. Anyway,
on any sensible calibrated scale of GCU eccentricity, such a
harmless, even benign prank would scarcely register.

I was sitting within sight of the door to Li'ndane's cabin. He
came out, chatting to Tel Ghemada. Li was flicking Brazil nuts into the air and running forward or bending over
backwards to catch them with his mouth, while trying to
carry on his side of the conversation. Tel was amused. Li
flicked one nut particularly far and had to dive and twist
under its trajectory, crashing into the floor and sliding into
the stool I had my feet up on (and yes, I do always loaf
a lot onboard ships; no idea why). Li rolled over on his
back, making a show of looking around him for the Brazil
nut. He looked mystified. Tel shook her head, smiling, then
waved goodbye. She was one of the unfortunates trying to
get some sort of human grasp of Earth's economics, and
deserved all the light relief she could get. I recall that all
through that year you could tell the economists by their
distraught look and slightly glazed-looking eyes. Li…well,
Li was just a wierdo, and forever conducting a running
battle with the finer sensibilities of the ship.

"Thank you, Li," I said, putting my feet back on the upended
stool. Li lay breathing heavily on the floor and looking up
at me, then his lips parted in a grin to reveal the nut caught

between his teeth. He swallowed, stood, pulled his pants halfway down, and proceeded to relieve himself against the trunk of the tree.

"Good for the growth," he said when he saw me frowning at him.

"Won't be any good for your growth if the ship catches you and sends a knife missile to sort you out."

"I can see what Mr. 'ndane is doing and I wasn't going to dignify his actions with as much as a comment," said a small drone, floating down from the foliage. It was one of a few drones the ship had built to follow a couple of birds that had been in the palm when it was hoisted up to the ship; the birds had to be fed, and tidied up after (the ship was proud that so far every dropping had been neatly intercepted in mid-air). "But I do admit I find his behaviour slightly worrying. Perhaps he wants to tell us what he feels about Earth, or me, or worse still, perhaps he doesn't know himself."

"Simpler than that," Li said, putting his dick away. "I needed a piss." He bent down and ruffled my hair before plonking himself down at my side.

("Urinal in your room packed up, has it?" muttered the drone. "Can't say I blame it...")

"I hear you're off back to the wilderness again tomorrow," Li said, crossing his arms and looking seriously at me. "I'm free this evening; in fact I'm free now. I could offer you a small token of my esteem if you like; your last night with the good guys before you go off to infiltrate the barbarians."

"Small?" I said.

Li smiled, made an expansive gesture, with both hands. "Well, modesty forbids..."

"No, I do."

"You're making a dreadful mistake you know," he said, jumping up and rubbing his belly absently while looking in the direction of the nearest dining area. "I'm in really fine form at the moment, and I really ain't doing anything tonight."

"Too right you aren't."

He shrugged and blew me a kiss, then skipped off. Li was one of those who just wouldn't have passed for Earth-human without a vast amount of physical alteration (hairy, and the wrong shape; imagine Quasimodo crossed with an ape), but frankly I think you could have put him down looking as normal as an IBM salesman and he'd still have been in jail or a fight within the hour; he couldn't have accepted the limitations on one's behaviour a place like Earth tends to insist on.

Denied his chance to go amongst the people of Earth, Li gave informal briefings for the people who were going down to the surface; those who would listen anyway. Li's briefings were short and to the point; he walked up, said, "The fundamental thing to remember is this; most of what you encounter will be shit."* And walked away again.

"Ms. Sma..." The small drone floated over and settled into the hollow left by Li's behind. "I was wondering if you would do me a small favour when you go back down tomorrow."

"What sort of favour?" I said, putting Regan and Goneril down.

"Well, I'd be terribly grateful if you'd call in at Paris before you go to Berlin...if you wouldn't mind."

"I...don't mind," I said. I hadn't been to Paris yet.

"Oh good."

"What's the problem?"

"No problem. I'd just like you to drop in on Dervley Linter. I think you know him? Well, just pop by for a chat, that's all."

"Uh-huh," I said.

I wondered what the ship was up to. I did have an idea (wrong, as it turned out). The *Arbitrary*, like every ship I've ever met in Contact, loved intrigues and plots. The devices

---

* Just a less precise re-statement of Sturgeon's Law.—"The Drone"

are forever using their spare time to cook up pranks and schemes; little secret plans, opportunities to use delicate artifices to get people to do things, say things, behave in a certain way, just for the fun of it. The *Arbitrary* was a notorious match-maker, perfectly convinced that it knew exactly who would be best for each other, always trying to fix the crew placements to set up as many potential couples or other suitable combinations as it could. It occurred to me that it was up to something like this now, worried that I hadn't been sexually active recently, and perhaps also concerned that my last few partners had been female (the *Arb* always did have a distinctly heterosexual bent for some reason).

"Yes, just a little talk; find out how things are going, you know."

The drone started to rise from the seat. I reached out and grabbed it, set it down on *Lear* on my lap, fixed its sensing band with what I hoped was a steely glare of my own and said, "What are you up to?"

"Nothing!" the machine protested. "I'd just like you to look in on Dervley and see what the two of you think about Earth, together; get a synthesis, you know. You two haven't met since we arrived and I want to see what ideas you can come up with...exactly how we should go about contacting them if that's what we decide to do, or what else we can do if we decide not to. That's all. No skullduggery, dear Sma."

"Hmm," I nodded. "All right."

I let the drone go. It floated up.

"Honest," the ship said, and the drone's aura field flashed rosy with bonhomie; "no skullduggery." It made a bobbing motion, indicating the book on my lap. "You read your *Lear*, I'll jet off."

A bird flashed by, closely followed by another drone; the one I'd been talking to tore off in pursuit. I shook my head. Competing for bird shit, already.

I watched the bird and the two machines dart down a corridor like the remains of some bizarre dogfight, then went
back to...

*Scene IV. The French camp. A tent.*
*Enter with drum and colours, Cordelia, Doctor, and soldiers.*

## 3: Helpless In The Face Of Your Beauty

*3.1: Synchronize Your Dogmas*

Now, the *Arbitrary* wasn't actually insane; it did its job very
well, and as far as I know none of its pranks ever actually
hurt anybody, at least not physically. But you have to be a
bit wary of a ship that collects snowflakes.

Put it down to its upbringing. The *Arb* was a product of one
of the manufactures in the Yinang Orbitals in the Dahass-
Khree. I've checked, and those factories have produced a
good per cent of the million or so GCUs there are blat-
ting about the place. That's quite a few craft*, and as far
as I can see, they're all a bit crazy. It must be the Minds
there I suppose; they seem to like turning out eccentric
ships. Shall I name names? See if you've heard of any of
this lot and their little escapades: The… *Cantankerous, Only
Slightly Bent, I Thought He Was With You, Space Monster, A
Series Of Unlikely Explanations, Big Sexy Beast, Never Talk To
Strangers, It'll Be Over By Christmas**, Funny, It Worked Last
Time…Boo!, Ultimate Ship The Second…*etc etc. Need I say
more?

Anyway, true to form, the *Arbitrary* had a little surprise for
me when I walked into the top hangar space the next
morning.

---

* About ten thousand, of course. Ms. Sma's mental arithmetic never was
too hot.—"The Drone"
** This is an extremely strained translation, but it's the best available.
                                                          —"The Drone"

Dawn was sweeping like an unrolled carpet of light and shadow over the Northern European Plain and pinking the snowy peaks of the Alps while I walked along the main corridor to the Bay, yawning and checking my passport and other papers (at least partly to annoy the ship; I knew damn well it wouldn't have made any mistakes), and making sure the drone following me had all my luggage.

I stepped into the hangár and was immediately confronted by a large red Volvo station wagon. It sat gleaming in the midst of the collection of modules, drones and platforms. I wasn't in the mood to argue, so I let the drone deposit my gear in the back and went to sit in the driver's seat, shaking my head. There was nobody else about. I waved goodbye to the drone as the automobile lifted gently into the air and made its way to the rear of the ship over the tops of the other devices in the Bay. They glittered in the brightness of the hangar lights as the big estate, wheels sagging, was pushed above them to the doorfields, and then into space.

The Bay door started to move back into place as we dropped beneath it and turned. The door slid into place, cutting off the light from the Bay; I was in perfect darkness for a moment, then the ship switched on the auto's lights.

"Ah, Sma?" the ship said from the stereo.

"What?"

"Seatbelt."

I remember sighing. I think I shook my head again, too.

We dropped in blackness, still inside the ship's inner field. As we finished turning, the Volvo's headlights picked out the slab-sided length of the *Arbitrary*, showing a very dull white inside its darkfield. Actually it was quite impressive, and oddly calming.

The ship killed the lights as we left the outer field. Suddenly I was in real space, the great gulf of spangled black before me, the planet like some vast droplet of water beneath, swirled with the pinpoint lights of Central and South America. I could make out San José, Panamá City, Bogotá and Quito. I looked back, but even knowing the ship was there I could see no sign that the stars it showed on its field skin weren't real.

I always did that, and always felt the same twinge of regret, even fear, knowing I was leaving our safe haven…but I soon settled, and enjoyed the trip down, riding through the atmosphere in my absurd motor car. The ship switched on the stereo again, and played me "Serenade" by the Steve Miller Band. Somewhere over the Atlantic, off Portugal I think, and just at the line, "The sun comes up, and shines all around me…" guess what happened?

All I can suggest is that you look again at some picture of it, half black with a billion scattered lights and streaks of dawning colour; I can't describe it further. We fell quickly. The car landed in the middle of some old coal workings in the unlovely north of France, near Béthune. By that time it was fully light. The field around the car popped and the two small platforms under the auto appeared, white slivers in the misty morning. They disappeared with their own "pop"s as the ship displaced them.

I drove to Paris. Living in Kensington I'd had a smaller car, a VW Golf, and the Volvo was like a tank after that. The ship spoke through my terminal brooch telling me which route to take to Paris, and then guided me through the streets to Linter's place. Even so it was a slightly traumatic experience because the whole city seemed snarled up with some cycle race, so when I eventually arrived in the courtyard just off the Boulevard St. Germain, where Linter had an apartment, I was in no mood to find that he wasn't there.

"Well, where the hell *is* he?" I demanded, standing on the balcony outside the apartment, hands on hips, glaring at the locked door. It was a sunny day, getting hot.

"I don't know," the ship said through the brooch.

I looked down at the thing, for all the good that did. "*What?*"

"Dervley has taken to leaving his terminal in his apartment when he goes out."

"He—" I stopped there, took a few deep breaths, and sat down on the steps. I switched my terminal off.

Something was going on. Linter was still here in Paris, despite the fact that this was where he'd been sent originally; his stay here shouldn't have been any longer than mine in London. Nobody on the ship had seen him since we'd first arrived; it looked like he hadn't been back to the ship at all. All the rest of us had. Why was he staying on here? And what was he thinking of, going out without taking his terminal? It was the act of a madman; what if something happened to him? What if he got knocked down in the street? (This seemed quite likely, judging from the standard of Parisian driving I'd encountered.) Or beaten up in a fight? And why was the ship treating all this so matter-of-factly? Going out without your terminal was acceptable enough on some cosy Orbital, and positively commonplace in a Rock or onboard ship, but *here*? Like taking a stroll through a game park without a gun...and just because the natives did it all the time didn't make it any less crazy.

I was quite certain now there was much more to this little jaunt to Paris than the ship had led me to believe. I tried to get some more information out of the beast, but it stuck to its ignorant act and so I gave up and left the car in the courtyard while I went for a walk.

I walked down the St. Germain until I came to the St. Michel, then headed for the Seine. The weather was bright and warm, the shops busy, the people as cosmopolitan as they were in London, if a little more stylishly dressed, on average. I think I was disappointed at first; the place wasn't that different. You saw the same products, the same signs; Mercedes-Benz, Westinghouse, American Express, De Beers, and so on...but gradually a more animated flavour of the city came through. A little more of Miller's Paris (I'd zipped through the *Tropics* the previous evening, as well as crossing them that morning), even if it was a little tamed with the passing of the years.

It was a different mix, another blend of the same ingredients; the traditional, the commercial, the nationalist...I rather liked the language. I could just about make myself understood, at a fairly low level (my accent was *formidable*, the ship had assured me), and could more or less read all the signs and advertisements...but spoken at the standard rate I couldn't make out more than one word in ten. So the language in the mouths of those *Parisiens* was like music, one unbroken flow of sound.

On the other hand, the populace seemed very reluctant to use any other language save their own even when they were technically able to, and if anything there seemed to be even fewer people in Paris willing and able to speak English than there were Londoners likewise equipped to tackle French. Post-Imperial snobbishness, perhaps.

In the shadow of Notre Dame I stood, thinking hard as I looked at that dull froth of brown stone which is the façade (I didn't go in; I was fed up with cathedrals, and by that time even my interest in castles was flagging). The ship wanted me to talk with Linter, for reasons I couldn't understand and it wasn't prepared to explain. Nobody had seen the guy, nobody had been able to call him, and nobody had received a message from him all the time we'd been over Earth. What had happened to him? And what was I supposed to do about it?

I walked along the banks of the Seine with all that cluttered, heavy architecture around me, and wondered.

I remembered the smell of roasting coffee (coffee was soaring in price at the time; them and their Commodities!), and the light that struck off the cobbles as little men turned on taps inside the sidewalks to wash the streets. They used old rags slung in front of the kerbs to divert the water this way and that.

For all my fruitless pondering, it was still wonderful to be there; there *was* something different about the city, something that really did make you feel glad to be alive.

Somehow I found my way to the upstream end of the Ile de Cité, although I'd meant to head towards the Pompidou Centre and then double back and cross by the Pont des Arts. There was a little triangular park at the island end, like some green fore-castle on a seaship, prow-facing those big-city waters of the dirty old Seine.

I walked into the park, hands in pockets, just wandering, and found some curiously narrow and austere—almost threatening—steps leading down between masses of rough-surfaced white stone. I hesitated, then went down, as though towards the river. I found myself in an enclosed courtyard; the only other exit I could see was down a slope to the water, but that was barred by a jagged construction of black steel. I felt uneasy. There was something about the hard geometry of the place that induced a sense of threat, of smallness and vulnerability; those jutting weights of white stone somehow made you think of how delicately crushable human bones were. I seemed to be alone. I stepped, reluctantly inquisitive, into the dark, narrow doorway that led back underneath the sunlit park.

It was the memorial to the Deportation.

I remember a thousand tiny lights, in rows, down a grilled-off tunnel, a recreated cell, fine words embossed…but I was in a daze. It's over a century ago now, but I still feel the cold of that place; I speak these words and a chill goes up my back; I edit them on screen and the skin on my arms, calves and flanks goes tight.

The effect remains as sharp as it was at the time; the details were as hazy a few hours afterwards as they are now, and as they will be until the day I die.

*3.2: Just Another Victim Of The Ambient Morality*

I came out stunned. I was angry at them, then. Angry at them for surprising me, touching me like that. Of course

I was angry at their stupidity, their manic barbarity, their unthinking, animal obedience, their appalling cruelty; everything that the memorial evoked...but what really hit me was that these people could create something that spoke so eloquently of their own ghastly actions; that they could fashion a work so humanly redolent of their own inhumanity. I hadn't thought them capable of that, for all the things I'd read and seen, and I didn't like to be surprised.

I left the island and walked along the right bank down towards the Louvre, and wandered through its galleries and halls, seeing but not seeing, just trying to calm down again. I glanded a little *softnow** to help the process along, and by the time I came to the Mona Lisa I was quite composed again. The *Giaconda* was a disappointment; too small and brown and surrounded by people and cameras and security. The lady smiled serenely from behind thick glass.

I couldn't find a seat and my feet were getting sore, so I wandered out into the Tuileries, along broad and dusty avenues between small trees, and eventually found a bench by an octagonal pond where small boys and their *pères* sailed model yachts. I watched them.

Love. Maybe it was love. Could that be it? Had Linter fallen for somebody, and was the ship therefore concerned he might not want to leave, if and when we had to? Just because that was the start of a thousand sentimental stories didn't mean that it didn't actually happen.

I sat by the octagonal pond, thinking about all this, and the same wind that ruffled my hair made the sails of the little yachts flutter and flap, and in that uncertain breeze they nosed through the choppy waters, and banged into the wall of the pond, or were caught by chubby hands and sent bobbing back out again across the waves.

I circled back via the Invalides, with more predictable trophies of war; old Panther tanks, and rows of ancient cannons like

* Effectively untranslatable.—"The Drone"

bodies stacked against a wall. I had lunch in a smoky little place near the St. Sulpice Metro; you sat on high stools at a bar and they selected a piece of red meat for you and put it, dripping blood, on a grid over an open pit filled with burning charcoal. The meat sizzled on the grill right in front of you while you had your *aperitif*, and you told them when you felt it was ready. They kept going to take it off and serve it to me, and I kept saying, *"Non non; un peu plus...s'il vous plait."* The man next to me ate his rare, with blood still oozing from the centre. After a few years in Contact you get used to that sort of thing, but I was still surprised I could sit there and do that, especially after the memorial. I knew so many people who'd have been outraged at the very thought. Come to think of it, there would have been millions of vegetarians on Earth who'd have been equally disgusted (would they have eaten our vat-grown meats? I wonder).

The black grill over the charcoal pit kept reminding me of the gratings in the memorial, but I just kept my head down and ate my meal, or most of it. I had a couple of glasses of rough red wine too, which I let have some effect, and by the time I was finished I was feeling reasonably together again, and quite well disposed to the locals. I even remembered to pay without being asked (I don't think you ever quite get used to *buying*), and went out into the bright sunshine. I walked back to Linter's, looking at shops and buildings and trying not to get knocked down in the street. I bought a paper on the way back, to see what our unsuspecting hosts thought was newsworthy. It was oil. Jimmy Carter was trying to persuade Americans to use less petrol, and the Norwegians had a blow-out in the North Sea. The ship had mentioned both items in its more recent synopses, but of course *it* knew Carter's measures weren't going to get through without drastic amendment, and that the drilling rig had had a piece of equipment fitted upside down. I selected a magazine as well, so arrived back at Linter's clutching my copy of *Stern* and expecting to have to drive

away. I'd already made tentative plans; going to Berlin via
the First World War graves and the old battle grounds, following the theme of war, death and memorials all the way
to the riven capital of the Third Reich itself.

But Linter's car was there in the courtyard, parked beside the
Volvo. His auto was a Rolls Royce Silver Cloud; the ship
believed in indulging us. Anyway, it claimed that making
a show was better cover than trying to stay inconspicuous;
Western capitalism in particular allowed the rich just about
the right amount of behavioural leeway to account for the
oddities our alienness might produce.

I went up the steps and pressed the bell. I waited for a short
while, hearing noises within the flat. A small notice on the
far side of the courtyard caught my attention, and brought
a sour smile to my face.

Linter appeared, unsmiling, at the door; he held it open for
me, bowing a little.

"Ms. Sma. The ship told me you'd be coming."

"Hello." I entered.

The apartment was much larger than I'd anticipated. It smelled
of leather and new wood; it was light and airy and well
decorated and full of books and records, tapes and magazines, paintings and *objets d'art*, and it didn't look one little
bit like the place I'd had in Kensington. It felt lived in.

Linter waved me towards a black leather chair at one end of
a Persian carpet covering a teak floor and went over to a
drinks cabinet, turning his back to me. "Do you drink?"

"Whisky," I said, in English. "With or without the 'e.'" I
didn't sit down, but wandered around the room, looking.

"I have Johnnie Walker Black Label."

"Fine."

I watched him clamp one hand round the square bottle and
pour. Dervley Linter was taller than me, and quite mus-
cular. To an experienced eye there was something not
quite right—in Earth human terms—about the set of his
shoulders. He leaned over the bottles and glasses like a

threat, as though he wanted to bully the drink from one to the other.

"Anything in it?"

"No thanks."

He handed me the glass, bent to a small fridge, extracted a bottle and poured himself a Budweiser (the real stuff, from Czechoslovakia). Finally, this little ceremony over, he sat down. Bahaus chair, and it looked original.

His face was calm, serious. Each feature seemed to demand separate attention; the large, mobile mouth, the flared nose, the bright but deep-set eyes, the stage-villain brows and surprisingly lined forehead. I tried to recall what he'd looked like before, but could only remember vaguely, so it was impossible to tell how much of the way he looked now had been carried over from what would be classed as his "normal" appearance. He rolled the beer glass around in his large hands.

"The ship seems to think we should talk," he said. He drank about half the beer in one gulp and placed the glass on a small table made of polished granite. I adjusted my brooch. "You don't think we should though, no?"

He spread his hands wide, then folded them over his chest. He was dressed in two pieces of an expensive looking black suit; trousers and waistcoat. "I think it might be pointless."

"Well...I don't know...does there have to be a point to everything? I thought...the ship suggested we might have a talk, that's—"

"Did it?"

"—all. Yes." I coughed. "I don't...it didn't tell me what's going on."

Linter looked steadily at me, then down at his feet. Black brogues. I looked around the room as I sipped my whisky, looking for signs of female habitation, or for anything that might indicate there were two people living here. I couldn't tell. The room was crowded with stuff; prints and oils on the walls, most of the former either Breughels or Lowrys;

Tiffany lampshades, a Bang and Olafsen Hi-fi unit, several antique clocks, what looked like a dozen or so Dresden figurines, a Chinese cabinet of black lacquer, a large four-fold screen with peacocks sewn onto it, the myriad feathers like displayed eyes...

"What *did* it tell you?" Linter asked.

I shrugged. "What I said. It said it wanted me to have a talk with you."

He smiled in an unimpressed sort of way as though the whole conversation was hardly worth the effort, then looked away, through the window. He didn't seem to be going to say anything. A flash of colour caught my eye, and I looked over at a large television, one of those with small doors that close over the screen and make it look like a cabinet when it isn't in use. The doors weren't fully shut, and it was switched on behind them.

"Do you want—?" Linter said.

"No, it's—" I began, but he rose out of the seat, gripping its elegant arms, went to the set and spread its doors open with a dramatic gesture before resuming his seat.

I didn't want to sit and watch television, but the sound was down so it wasn't especially intrusive. "The control unit's on the table," Linter said, pointing.

"I wish you—somebody—wish you'd tell me what's going on."

He looked at me as though this was an obvious lie rather than a genuine plea, and glanced over at the TV. It must have been on one of the ship's own channels, because it was changing all the time, showing different shows and programmes from a variety of countries, using various transmission formats, and waiting for a channel to be selected. A group in bright pink suits danced mechanically to an unheard song. They were replaced with a picture of the Ekofisk platform, spouting a dirty brown fountain of oil and mud. Then the screen changed again, to show the crowded cabin scene from *A Night At The Opera*.

"So you don't know anything?" Linter lit a Sobranie. This, like the ship's "Hmm," had to be for effect (unless he liked the taste, which has never been a convincing line). He didn't offer me one.

"No, no, no I don't. Look...I can see the ship wanted me here for more than this talk...but don't you play games too. That crazy thing sent me down here in that Volvo; the whole way. I half expected it not to have baffled it either; I was waiting for a pair of Mirages to come to intercept. I've got a long drive to Berlin as well, you know? So...just tell me, or tell me to go, all right?"

He drew on the cigarette, studying me through the smoke. He crossed his legs and brushed some imaginary fluff off the trouser cuffs and stared at his shoes. "I've told the ship that when it leaves, I'm staying here on Earth. Regardless of what else might happen." He shrugged. "Whether we contact or not." He looked at me, challenging.

"Any...particular reason?" I tried to sound unfazed. I still thought it must be a woman.

"Yes. I like the place." He made a noise between a snort and a laugh. "I feel alive for a change. I want to stay. I'm going to. I'm going to live here."

"You want to die here?"

He smiled, looked away from me, then back. "Yes." Quite positively. This shut me up for a moment.

I felt uncomfortable. I got up and walked round the room, looking at the bookshelves. He seemed to have read about the same amount as me. I wondered if he'd crammed it all, or read any of it at normal speed: Dostoevsky, Borges, Greene, Swift, Lucretius, Kafka, Austen, Grass, Bellow, Joyce, Confucius, Scott, Mailer, Camus, Hemingway, Dante. "You probably will die here, then," I said lightly. "I suspect the ship wants to observe, not contact. Of course—"

"That'll suit me. Fine."

"Hmm. Well, it isn't...official yet, but I...that's the way it'll go, I suspect." I turned away from the books. "It *does*? You really want to die here? Are you serious? How—"

He was sitting forward in the chair, combing his black hair
with one hand, pushing the long, ringed fingers through
his curls. A silver stud decorated the lobe of his left ear.

"Fine," he repeated. "It'll suit me perfectly. We'll ruin this
place if we interfere."

"They'll ruin it if we don't."

"Don't be trite, Sma." He stubbed the cigarette out hard,
breaking it in half, mostly unsmoked.

"And if they blow the place up?"

"Mmm."

"Well?"

"Well what?" he demanded.

A siren sounded on the St. Germain, dopplering. "Might be
what they're heading for. Want to see them moth themselves in front of their own—"

"Ah, bullshit." His face crinkled with annoyance.

"Bullshit yourself," I told him. "Even the ship's worried. The
only reason they haven't made a final decision yet is because
they know how bad it'll look short term if they do."

"Sma, I don't care. I don't want to leave. I don't want to have
any more to do with the ship or the Culture or anything
connected with it."

"You must be crazy. As crazy as they are. They'll kill you;
you'll get crushed under a truck or mangled in a plane crash
or…burned up in some fire or something…"

"So I take my chances."

"Well…what about what they'd call the 'security' aspect?
What if you're only injured and they take you to hospital?
You'll never get out again; they'll take one look at your guts
or your blood and they'll know you're alien. You'll have the
military all over you. They'll *dissect* you."

"Not very likely. But if it happens, it happens."

I sat down again. I was reacting just the way the ship had
known I would. I thought Linter was mad just the way
the *Arbitrary* did, and it was using me to try and talk some
sense into him. Doubtless the ship had already tried, but

equally obviously the nature of Linter's decision was such that the *Arbitrary* was the last thing that was going to have any influence. Technologically and morally the ship represented the most finely articulated statement the Culture was capable of producing, and that very sophistication had the beast hamstrung, here.

I have to admit I felt a degree of admiration for Linter's stand, even though I still thought he was being stupid. There might or might not be a local involved, but I was already getting the impression it was more complicated—and more difficult to handle—than that. Maybe he had fallen in love, but not with anything as simple as a person. Maybe he'd fallen in love with Earth itself; the whole fucking planet. So much for Contact screening; they were supposed to keep people out who might fall like that. If that was what had happened then the ship had problems indeed. Falling in love with somebody, they say, is a little like getting a tune into your head and not being able to stop whistling it…except much more so, and—from what I'd heard—going native the way I suspected Linter might be was as far beyond loving another person as that was beyond getting a tune stuck in your head.

I felt suddenly angry, at Linter and the ship.

"I think you're taking a very selfish and stupid risk that's not just bad for you, and bad for the…for us; for the Culture, but also bad for these people. If you do get caught, if you're discovered…they *are* going to get paranoid, and they might feel threatened and hostile in any contact they are involved, in or ex. You could send them…make them crazy. Insane."

"You said they were that already."

"And you *do* stand a less chance of living your full term. Even if you don't; so you live for centuries. How d'you explain that?"

"They may have anti-geriatrics themselves by that time. Besides, I can always move around."

"They won't have anti-geriatrics for fifty years or more; centuries if they relapse, even without a Holocaust. Yeah; so
move around, make yourself a fugitive, stay alien, stay apart.
You'll be as cut off from them as you will be from us. Ah
hell, you always will be anyway." I was talking loudly by now. I
waved one arm at the bookshelves. "Sure read the books and
see the films and go to concerts and theatre and opera and all
that shit; you can't *become* them. You'll still have Culture eyes,
Culture brain; you can't just...can't deny all that, pretend it
never happened." I stamped one foot on the floor. "God *dammit*, Linter, you're just being ungrateful!"

"Listen, Sma," he said, rising out of the seat, grabbing his beer
and stalking about the room, gazing out of the windows.
"Neither of us owes the Culture anything. You know that...
Owing and being obliged and having duties and responsibilities and everything like that...that's what *these* people
have to worry about." He turned round to look at me. "But
not me, not us. You do what you want to do, the ship does
what it wants to do. I do what I want to do. All's well. Let's
just leave each other alone, yes?" He looked back at the
small courtyard, finishing his beer.

"You want to be like them, but you don't want to have their
responsibilities."

"I didn't say I wanted to be like them. To...to whatever extent
I do, I want to have the same sort of responsibilities, and
that doesn't include worrying about what a Culture starship
thinks. That isn't something any of them normally tend to
worry about."

"What if Contact surprises us both, and does come in?"

"I doubt that."

"Me too, very much; that's why I think it might happen."

"I don't think so. Though it is we who need them, not the
other way round." Linter turned and stared at me, but I
wasn't going to start arguing on a second front now. "But,"
he said after a pause, "the Culture can do without me." He
inspected his drained glass. "It's going to have to."

I was silent for a while, watching the television flip through
channels. "What about you though?" I asked eventually.
"Can you do without it?"
"Easily," Linter laughed. "Listen, d'you think I haven't—"
"No; you listen. How long do you think this place is going
to stay the way it is now? Ten years? Twenty? Can't you see
how much this place has to alter...in just the next century?
We're so used to things staying much the same, to society
and technology—at least immediately available technology—
hardly changing over our lifetimes that...I don't know any
of us could cope for long down here. I think it'll affect you
a lot more than the locals. They're used to change, used to it
all happening fast. All right, you like the way it is now, but
what happens later? What if 2077 is as different from now
as this is from 1877? This might be the end of a Golden
Age, world war or not. What chance do *you* think the West
has of keeping the status quo with the Third World? I'm
telling you; end of the century and you'll feel lonely and
afraid and wonder why they've deserted you and you'll be
the worst nostalgic they've got because you'll remember it
better than they ever will and you won't remember anything else from before now."
He just stood looking at me. The TV showed part of a ballet
in black and white, then an interview; two white men who
looked American somehow (and the fuzzy picture looked
U.S. standard), then a quiz show, then a puppet show, again
in monochrome. You could see the strings. Linter put his
glass down on the granite table and went over to the Hi-fi,
turning on the tape deck. I wondered what little bit of planetary accomplishment I was going to be treated to.
The picture on the screen settled to one programme for a
while. It looked vaguely familiar; I was sure I'd seen it.
A play; last century...American writer, but...(Linter went
back to his seat, while the music began; the *Four Seasons*.)
Henry James, *The Ambassadors*. It was a TV production I'd
seen on the BBC while I was in London...or maybe the

ship had repeated it. I couldn't recall. What I did recall was the plot and the setting, both of which seemed so apposite to my little scene with Linter that I started to wonder whether the beast upstairs was watching all this. Probably was, come to think of it. And not much point in looking for anything; the ship could produce bugs so small the main problem with camera stability was Brownian motion. Was *The Ambassadors* a sign from it then? Whatever; the play was replaced by a commercial for Odor-Eaters.

"I've told you," Linter brought me back from my musings, speaking quietly, "I'm prepared to take my chances. Do you think I haven't thought it all through before, many times? This isn't sudden, Sma; I felt like this my first day here, but I waited for months before I said anything, so I'd be sure. It's what I've been looking for all my life, what I've always wanted. I always knew I'd know it when I found it, and I have." He shook his head; sadly, I thought. "I'm staying, Sma."

I shut up. I suspected that despite what he'd just said he hadn't thought about how much the planet would change during his long likely lifetime, and there were still other things to be said, but I didn't want to press too hard too quickly. I made myself relax on the couch and shrugged. "Anyway, we don't know for sure what the ship's going to do; what they'll decide."

He nodded, picked up a paperweight from the granite table and turned it over and over in his hand. The music shimmered through the room, like the sun on water reflected; points producing lines, dancing quietly. "I know," he said, still gazing at the heavy globe of twisted glass, "this must seem like a mad idea...but I just...just *want* the place." He looked at me—for the first time, I thought—without a challenging scowl or stern coolness.

"I know what you mean," I said. "But I can't understand it perfectly...maybe I'm more suspicious than you are; it's just you tend to be more concerned for other people than for yourself sometimes...you assume they haven't thought things through the way you would have yourself." I sighed, almost laughed. "I guess I'm assuming you'll...hoping you'll change your mind."

Linter was silent for a while, still studying the hemisphere of coloured glass. "Maybe I will." He shrugged massively. "Maybe I will," he said, looking at me speculatively. He coughed. "Did the ship tell you I've been to India?"

"India? No; no, it didn't."

"I went there for a couple of weeks. I didn't tell the *Arbitrary* I was going, though it found out, of course."

"Why? I mean why did you want to go?"

"I wanted to see the place," Linter said, sitting forward in the seat, rubbing the paperweight, then replacing it on the granite table and rubbing his palms together. "It was beautiful...beautiful. If I'd had any second thoughts, they vanished there." He looked at me, face suddenly open, intent, his hands outstretched, fingers wide. "It's the contrast, the..." He looked away, apparently made less articulate by the vividness of the impression. "...the highlights, the light and shade of it all. The squalor and the muck, the cripples and the swollen bellies; the whole poverty of it makes the beauty stand out...a single pretty girl in the crowds of Calcutta seems like an impossibly fragile bloom, like a... I mean you can't believe that the filth and the poverty hasn't somehow contaminated her...it's like a miracle... a revelation. Then you realize that she'll only be like that for a few years, that she'll only live a few decades, then she'll *wear* and have six kids and wither...The feeling, the realization, the staggering..." His voice trailed off and he looked, slightly helplessly, almost vulnerably, at me. It was just the point at which to make my most telling, cutting comment. But also just the point at which I could do no such thing.

So I sat still, saying nothing, and Linter said, "I don't know how to explain it. It's alive. I'm alive. If I did die tomorrow it would have been worth it just for these last few months. I know I'm taking a risk in staying, but that's the whole point. I *know* I might feel lonely and afraid. I expect that's going to happen, now and again, but it'll be worth it. The loneliness will *make* the rest worth it. We expect everything to be set up just as we like it, but these people don't; they're used to having good and bad mixed in together. And that gives them an interest in living, it makes them appreciate opportunities…these people know what tragedy is, Sma. They live it. We're just an audience." ›

He sat there, looking away from me, while I stared at him. The big-city noise grumbled beyond us, and the sunlight came and went in the room as shadows of clouds passed over us and I thought; you poor bastard, you poor schmuck, they've got you.

Here we are with our fabulous GCU, our supreme machine; capable of outgenerating their entire civilization and taking in Proxima Centauri on a day trip; packed with technology compared to which their citybusters are squibs and their Crays are less than calculators; a vessel casually sublime in its impregnable power and inexhaustible knowledge… here we are with our ship and our modules and platforms, satellites and scooters and drones and bugs, sieving their planet for its most precious art, its most sensitive secrets, its finest thoughts and greatest achievements; plundering their civilization more comprehensively than all the invaders in their history put together, giving not a damn for their puny armaments, paying a hundred times more attention to their art and history and philosophy than to their eclipsed science, glancing at their religions and politics the way a doctor would at symptoms…and for all that, for all our power and our superiority in scale, science, technology, thought and behaviour, here was this poor sucker, besotted with them when they didn't even know he existed, spellbound with them, adoring them; and powerless. An immoral victory for the barbarians.

Not that I was in a much better position myself. I may have wanted the exact opposite of Dervley Linter, but I very much doubted I was going to get my way, either. I didn't want to leave, I didn't want to keep them safe from us and let them devour themselves; I wanted maximum inter-ference; I wanted to hit the place with a programme Lev Davidovitch would have been proud of. I wanted to see the junta generals fill their pants when they realized that the future is—in Earth terms—bright, bright red.

Naturally the ship thought I was crazy too. Perhaps it imag-ined Linter and I would cancel each other out somehow, and we'd both be restored to sanity.

So Linter wanted nothing done to the place, and I wanted everything done to it. The ship—along with whatever other Minds were helping it decide what to do—was prob-ably going to come down closer to Linter's position than mine, but that was the very reason the man couldn't stay. He'd be a little randomly-set time bomb ticking away in the middle of the uncontaminated experiment that Earth was probably going to become; a parcel of radical contamina-tion ready to Heisenberg the whole deal at any moment.

There was nothing more I could do with Linter for the moment. Let him think about what I'd said. Perhaps just knowing it wasn't only the ship that thought he was being foolish and selfish would make some difference.

I got him to show me around Paris in the Rolls, then we ate—magnificently—in Montmartre, and ended up on the Left Bank, wandering the maze of streets and sampling a prof-ligate number of wines and spirits. I had a room booked at the George, but stayed with Linter that night, just because it seemed the most natural thing to do—especially in that drunken state—and anyway it had been a while since I'd had somebody to hug during the night.

Next morning, before I set off for Berlin, we both exhib-ited just the right amount of embarrassment, and so parted friends.

*3.3: Arrested Development*

There is something about the very idea of a city which is
central to the understanding of a planet like Earth, and particularly the understanding of that part of the then-existing
group-civilization* which called itself the West. That idea,
to my mind, met its materialist apotheosis in Berlin at the
time of the Wall.

Perhaps I go into some sort of shock when I experience something deeply; I'm not sure, even at this ripe middle-age, but
I have to admit that what I recall of Berlin is not arranged
in my memory in any normal, chronological sequence. My
only excuse is that Berlin itself was so abnormal—and yet
so bizarrely representative—it was like something unreal;
an occasionally macabre Disneyworld which was so much a
part of the real world (and the *realpolitik* world), so much
a crystallization of everything these people had managed
to produce, wreck, reinstate, venerate, condemn and wor-
ship in their history that it defiantly transcended everything it exemplified, and took on a single—if multifariously
faceted—meaning of its own; a sum, an answer, a statement
no city in its right mind would want or be able to arrive at.
I said we were more interested in Earth's art than anything
else; very well, Berlin was its masterpiece, an equivalent for
the ship.

I remember walking round the city, day and night, seeing
buildings whose walls were still pocked with bullet holes
from a war ended thirty-two years earlier. Lit, crowded,
otherwise ordinary office buildings looked as though they'd
been sandblasted with grains the size of tennis balls; police
stations, apartment blocks, churches, park walls, the very
sidewalks themselves bore the same stigmata of ancient
violence, the mark of metal on stone.

---

* Another tricky one. Ms. Sma keeps on using words there is no direct
English equivalent for.—"The Drone"

I could *read* those walls; reconstruct from that wreckage the
events of a day, or an afternoon, or an hour, or just a few
minutes. Here the machine-gun fire had sprayed, light
ordinance like acid pitting, heavier guns leaving tracks like
a succession of pickaxe blows on ice; here shaped-charge
and kinetic weapons had pierced—the holes had been
bricked up—and sprayed long rays of jagged holes across
the stone; here a grenade had exploded, fragments blast-
ing everywhere, shallow cratering the sidewalk and spraying the wall (or not; sometimes there was untouched stone
in one direction, like a shrapnel shadow, where perhaps
a soldier left his image on the city at the moment of his
death).

In one place all the marks, on a railway arch, were wildly
slanted, cutting a swathe across one side of the arch, hitting the pavement, then slanting up on the other side of
the alcove. I stood and wondered at that, then realized that
three decades before some Red Army soldier had probably
crouched there, drawing fire from a building across the
street...I turned, and could even see which window...

I took the West-operated U-bahn under the wall, cutting across
from one part of West Berlin to the other, from Hallesches
Tor to Tegel. At Friedrichstrasse you could quit the train
and enter East Berlin, but the other stations under East
were closed; guards with submachine guns stood watching
the train rush through the deserted stations; an eerie blue
glow lit this film-set of a scene, and the train's passing sent
ancient papers scattering, and lifted the torn corners of old
posters still stuck to the wall. I had to make that journey
twice, to be sure I hadn't imagined it all; the other passengers had looked as bored and zombie-like as underground
passengers usually do.

There was something of that frightening, ghostly emptiness
about the city itself at times. Although so surely enclosed,
West Berlin was big; full of parks and trees and lakes—more
so than most cities—and that, combined with the fact that

people were still leaving the city in their tens of thousands each year (despite all sorts of grants and tax concessions designed to persuade them to stay) meant that while there was the same quality of high capitalist presence I'd been immersed in in London and sensed in Paris, the density was much reduced; there simply wasn't the same pressure to develop and redevelop the land. So the city was full of those shot-up buildings and wide open spaces; bomb sites with shattered ruins on the skyline, empty-windowed and roofless like great abandoned ships adrift on seas of weeds. Alongside the elegance of the Kurfürstendamm, this legacy of destruction and privation became just another vast art work, like the quaintly shattered steeple of the Kaiser Wilhelm Memorial Church, set at the end of the K-damm like a folly at the end of an avenue of trees.

Even the two rail systems contributed to the sense of unreality the city inspired, the sense of continually stepping from one continuum to another. Instead of the West running everything on its side, and the East everything on its, the East ran the S-bahn (above ground) on both sides, the West the U-bahn (underground) on both sides; the U-bahn served those ghostly stations under the East and the S-bahn had its own tumbledown, weed-strewn stations in the West. Both ignored the wall, indeed, because the S-bahn went over the top of it. And the S-bahn went underground in places. And the U-bahn surfaced frequently. Let me labour the point and say that even double-decker buses and double-decker trains added to the sense of a multilayered reality. In a place like Berlin, wrapping the Reichstag up like a parcel wasn't even remotely as weird an idea as the city was itself.

I went once via Friedrichstrasse and once through Checkpoint Charlie, into the East. Sure enough, there were places where time seemed to have stopped there too, and many of the buildings and signs looked as though a patina of dust had started settling over them thirty years ago, and never been disturbed since. There were shops in the East where one could only spend foreign currency. Somehow they just didn't look like real shops; it was as though some seedy entrepreneur from a degenerate semi-socialist future had tried to create a fairground display modelled on a late twentieth-century capitalist shop, and failed, through lack of imagination.

It wasn't convincing. I wasn't convinced. I was a little shaken, too. Was this farce, this gloomy sideshow trying to mimic the West—and not even doing that very well—the best job the locals could make of socialism? Maybe there was something so basically wrong with them even the ship hadn't spotted it yet; some genetic flaw that meant they were never going to be able to live and work together without an external threat; never stop fighting, never stop making their awful, awesome, bloody messes. Perhaps despite all our resources there was nothing we *could* do for them.

The feeling passed. There was nothing to prove this wasn't just a momentary, and—coming so early—understandable aberration. Their history wasn't so far off the mean track, they were going through what a thousand other civilizations had gone through, and no doubt in the childhood of each of those there had been countless occasions when all any decent, well-balanced, reasonable and humanely concerned observer would have wanted to do was scream in despair.

It was ironic that in this so-called Communist capital they were so interested in money; at least a dozen people came up to me in the East and asked me if I wanted to change some. Would this represent a qualitative or quantitative change? I asked (blank looks, mostly). "Money implies poverty," I quoted them. Hell, they should engrave that in stone over the hangar door of every GCU.

I stayed for a month, visiting all the tourist haunts, walking and driving and training and busing through the city, sailing on and swimming in the Havel, and riding through Grunewald and Spandau forests.

I left by the Hamburg corridor, at the ship's suggestion. The road went through villages stuck in the fifties. The eighteen fifties, sometimes; chimney sweeps on bikes wore tall black hats and carried their black-caned brushes over their shoulders like huge sooty daisies stolen from a giant's garden. I felt quite self-conscious and rich in my big red Volvo.

I left the car on a track by the side of the Elbe that night. A module sighed out of the darkness, dark on dark, and took me to the ship, which was over the Pacific at the time, tracking a school of sperm whales directly beneath and plundering their great barrel-brains with its effectors while they sang.

## 4: Heresiarch

*4.1: Minority Report*

I should have known not to tell Li'ndane about Paris and Berlin, but I did. I was floating in the AG space with a few other people after a dip in the ship's pool. I'd actually been talking to my friends, Roghres Shasapt and Tagm Lokri, but Li was there, eavesdropping avidly.

"Ah," he said, floating over to wag one finger under my nose. "That's it."

"That's what?"

"That monument. I see it now. Think about it."

"The memorial to the Deportation, in Paris, you mean."

"Cunt. That's what I mean."

I shook my head. "Li, I don't think I know what you're talking about."

"Ah, he's just lusting," Roghres said. "He pined when you left last time."

"Nonsense," Li said, and flicked a blob of water at Roghres. "What I'm talking about is this; most memorials are like pricks; cenotaphs; columns. That monument Sma saw is a cunt; it's even in a divide of the river; very pubic. From this, and Sma's overall attitude, it's obvious that Sma is sublimating her sexuality in all this Contact nonsense."

"Well I never knew that," I said.

"Basically, what you want, Diziet, is to be fucked by an entire civilization, an entire planet. I suppose this makes you a good little Contact operative, if that's what you want to be—"

"Li, of course, is only here for the different tan," Tagm interrupted.

"—but I would say," Li continued, "that it's better not to sublimate anything. If what you want is a good *screw*—" (Li used the English word) "—then a good screw is what you ought to have, not a meaningful confrontation with a backwater rockball infested with slavering death-zealots on a terminal power trip."

"I still say it's you who wants the good screw," Roghres said.

"Exactly!" Li exclaimed, throwing his arms wide, scattering more water drops, wobbling in the null G. "But *I* don't deny it."

"Just Mr. Natural," Tagm nodded.

"What's wrong with being natural?" demanded Li.

"But I remember just the other day you were saying that the trouble with humans is that they were too natural, not civilized enough," Tagm said, then turned to me. "Mind you, that was then; Li can change his colours faster than a GCU going for a refit record."

"There's natural and natural," Li said. "I'm naturally civilized and they're naturally barbarians, therefore I should be as natural as possible and they should do all they can not to be. But this is getting off the subject. What I say is that Sma has a definite psychological problem and I think that as I'm the only person on this machine interested in Freudian analysis, I should be the one to help her."

"That's unbelievably kind of you," I told Li.

"Not at all," Li waved his hand. He must have scattered most of his water drops towards us, because he was gradually floating away from us, towards the far end of the AG hall.

"Freud!" snorted Roghres derisively, a little high on *Jumble*.

"You heathen," said Li, eyes narrowed. "I suppose your heroes are Marx and Lenin."

"Hell no; I'm an Adam Smith man myself," muttered Roghres. She started to tumble head over heels in the air, doing slow foetal-spreadeagle exercises.

"Rubbish," Li spat (literally, but I saw it coming and dodged).

"Li, you really are the horniest\* human on this ship," Tagm told him. "You're the one who needs the analyst. This obsession with sex, it's just not—"

"*I'm* obsessed with sex?" Li said, poking himself in the chest with a thumb, then throwing back his head. "HA!" He laughed. "Listen"; he arranged himself in what would have passed for a lotus position on Earth, had there been a floor to sit on, and put one hand on his hip while pointing the other vaguely to his right; "*they're* the ones obsessed with sex. Do you know how many words there are for 'prick' in English? Or 'cunt'? Hundreds; hundreds. How many have we got? One; one for each, for——\*\* usage as well as for anatomical designation. Neither of them swear-words. All I do is readily admit I want to put one in the other. Ready, willing and interested. What's wrong with that?"

"Nothing as such," I told him. "But there's a point where interest becomes obsession, and I think most people regard obsession as a bad thing because it makes for less variety, less flexibility."

Li, still floating slowly away from us, nodded fiercely. "I'll just say one thing; it's an obsession with flexibility and variety that makes this so-called Culture so boring."

"Li started a Boredom Society while you were away," Tagm explained, smiling at me. "Nobody else joined though."

"It's going very well," Li confirmed. "I've changed the title to the Ennui League, by the way. Yes, boredom is an under-rated facet of existence in our pseudo-civilization. While at first I thought it might be interesting, in a boring sense, for people to be together when they were extremely bored, I realize now that it is a profoundly moving and deeply average

---

\* Sma refuses to choose between British English and American English. This would be "randiest" in British English.—"The Drone"

\*\* The word Sma insists upon using is exactly midway in meaning between "common" and "vulgar." Take your pick.—"The Drone"

experience to do nothing whatsoever entirely and completely by yourself."

"You think Earth has a lot to teach us in this respect?" Tagm said, then turned and said to the nearest wall, "Ship, put the air on medium, would you?"

"Earth is a deeply boring planet," Li said gravely, as one end of the hall began to waft the air towards us, and the other turned intake. We began to drift in the breeze.

"Earth? Boring?" I said. The water was drying on my skin.

"What is the *point* of a planet where you can hardly set foot without tripping over somebody killing somebody else, or painting something or making music or pushing back the frontier of science or being tortured or killing themselves or dying in a car crash or hiding from the police or suffering from some absurd disease or—"

We hit the soft, porous intake wall ("Hey, this wall sucks!" Roghres giggled), and the three of us bounced, and passed Li, a little behind us and travelling in the opposite direction, still heading for the wall. Roghres watched him going by with the studied interest of a bar drunk watching a fly on the rim of a glass. "Far out."

"Anyway," I said, as we passed. "How does all this make it boring? Surely there's so much going on—"

"That it's deeply boring. An excess of boringness does not make a thing interesting except in the driest academic sense. A place is not boring if you have to look really hard for something which is interesting. If there is absolutely nothing interesting about any particular place, then that is a perfectly interesting and quintessentially un-boring place." Li hit the wall and bounced. We had slowed, stopped, and reversed, so were coming back down again. Roghres waved at Li as we passed him.

"But," I said, "Earth—let me get this right—Earth, where everything's happening, is so full of interesting things that it's boring." I squinted at Li. "Is that what you mean?"

"Something like that."

"You're crazy."
"You're boring."


*4.2: Happy Idiot Talk*

I'd talked to the ship about Linter the day after I saw him in
  Paris, and a few times subsequently. I don't think I was
  able to offer much hope that the man would change his
  mind; the ship used its Depressed voice when we talked
  about him.
Of course if the ship wanted to it could have made the whole
  argument academic by just kidnapping Linter. The more I
  thought about it, the more certain I became that the ship
  had bugs or microdrones or something trailing the man; at
  the first hint that he was thinking about staying the *Arbi-*
  *trary* would have made sure that it couldn't lose him, even
  when he went out without his terminal. For all I knew it
  watched all of us, though it protested that it didn't when
  I asked it (about Linter the ship was evasive, and there's
  nothing more slippery in the galaxy than a GCU being
  cagey, so a straight answer was out of the question.* But
  draw your own conclusions.)
Nothing would have been easier, technically, for the ship to
  drug Linter, or have a drone stun him, and bundle him
  into a module. I suppose it could even have displaced him;
  beamed him up like in *Star Trek* (which the ship thought was
  a great hoot).** But I couldn't see it doing anything like that.
I have yet to meet a ship—and I don't think I'd *like* to meet
  a ship—that didn't take far more pride in its mental abili-
  ties than its physical power, and for the ship to kidnap
  Linter would be an admission that it hadn't had the wit to

---

* I think this jars abominably, but herself disagrees.—"The Drone"
** Ms. Sma is confusing matter transmission (sic) with transdimensional
displacement of a remotely induced singularity. I despair.—"The Drone"

out-think the man. No doubt it would make the best possible job of justifying such an act if it did do it, and it would certainly get away with it—no quorum of other Contact Minds would offer it the choice of exile or restructuring—but boy would it lose face. GCUs can be bitchy as hell, and the *Arbitrary* would be the laughing-stock of the Contact fleet for months, minimum.

"Would you even think about it?"

"I *think* of everything," the ship replied tartly. "But no, I don't think I'd do it, even as a last resort."

A whole bunch of us had watched *King Kong* and now we were sitting by the ship's pool, snacking on *kazu* and sampling some French wines (all ship-grown, but statistically more authentic than the real thing, it assured us...No, me neither). I'd been thinking about Linter, and asked a remote drone what contingency plans had been made if it came to the worst.*

"What is the last resort?"

"I don't know; trail him perhaps, watch for a situation where the locals are about to find out he's not one of them—in a hospital, say—then micronuke the place."

"*What?*"

"It'd make a great Mystery Explosion story."

"Be serious."

"I'm being serious. What's one more meaningless act of violence on that zoo of a planet? It would be appropriate. When in Rome; burn it."

"You're not really being serious, are you?"

"Sma! Of course not! Are you on something, or what? Good grief, damn the morality of the thing: it would just be so *inelegant*. What do you take me for? Really!" The drone left.

---

* Actually, Sma was talking to a ship-slaved tray carrying drinks, but she thinks it sounds silly to say she was talking to a tray.

—"The Drone"

I dangled my feet in the pool. The ship was playing us thirties jazz, in untidied-up form; crackles and hisses left in. It had gone on to that and Gregorian chants after a period—when I'd been to Berlin—of trying to make everybody listen to Stockhausen. I wasn't sorry I'd missed that stage in the ship's constantly altering musical taste.

Also while I'd been away, the ship had sent a request on a post-card to the BBC's World Service, asking for "Mr. David Bowie's 'Space Oddity' for the good ship *Arbitrary* and all who sail in her." (This from a machine that could have swamped Earth's entire electromagnetic spectrum with whatever the hell it wanted from somewhere beyond Betel-geuse.) It didn't get the request played. The ship thought this was hilarious.

"Here's Dizzy; she'll know."

I turned round to see Roghres and Djibard Alsahil approach-ing. They sat down at my side. Djibard had been friendly with Linter in the year between leaving the *Bad For Busi-ness* and finding Earth.

"Hello," I said. "Know what?"

"What's happened to Dervley Linter?" Roghres said, trailing one hand in the pool. "Djib's just back from Tokyo and wanted to see him, but the ship's being awkward; won't say where he is."

I looked at Djibard, who was sitting cross-legged, looking like a little gnome. She was smiling broadly; she looked stoned.

"What makes you think I know anything?" I said to Roghres.

"I heard a rumour you'd seen him in Paris."

"Hmm. Well, yes, I did." I watched the pretty light patterns the ship was making on the far wall; they were slowly appearing brighter as the main lights went rosy with the ship's evening (which it had gradually brought down to a 24-hour cycle).

"So why hasn't he come back to the ship?" Roghres said. "He went to Paris right at the start. How come he's still there? Isn't going native is he?"

"I only saw him for a day; less, in fact. I wouldn't like to comment on his mental state...he seemed happy enough."

"Don't answer then," Djibard said, a little slurred.

I looked at Djibard for a moment; she was still smiling. I turned back to Roghres. "Why not contact him yourselves?"

"Tried that," Roghres said. She nodded at the other woman. "Djibard tried on- and off-planet. No reply."

Djibard's eyes were closed now. I looked at Roghres. "Then he probably doesn't want to talk."

"You know," Djibard said, eyes still closed, "I think it's because we don't mature the way they do. I mean the females have periods, and the men have this *machismo* thing because they've got to do all the things they're supposed to do and so we don't; I mean we don't have things they do...what I mean is that there are all sorts of things that do things to them, and we don't have that. Them. We don't have them and so we don't get *ground down* the way they do. I think that's the secret. Pressures and knocks and disappointments. I think that's what somebody said to me. But I mean it's so unfair...but I don't know who for yet; I haven't worked that out, you know?"

I looked at Roghres and she looked at me. Some drugs do turn you into a blabbering moron for the duration.

"I think you know something you're not telling us," Roghres said. "And I don't think I'm going to coax it out of you." She smiled. "I know; if you don't tell, I'll say to Li that you told me you're secretly in love with him and just playing hard to get. How about that?"

"I'll tell my mum, and she's bigger than yours."

Roghres laughed. She took Djibard by the hand and they both stood. They moved off, Roghres guiding Djibard, who as she moved away was saying, "You know, I think it's because we don't mature the way they do. I mean the females—"

A drone carrying empty glasses passed by and muttered, "Gibbering Djibard," in English. I smiled, and waggled my feet in the warm water.

*4.3: Ablation*

I was in Auckland for a couple of weeks, then Edinburgh, then back in the ship again. One or two people asked me about Linter, but obviously word got round that while I probably knew something, I wasn't going to tell anybody. Still, nobody seemed any less friendly because of that.

Meanwhile Li had embarked upon a campaign to get the ship to let him visit Earth without modification. His plan was to go mountain descending; have himself dropped on a summit and then make his way down. He told the ship that this would be perfectly safe security-wise, in the Himalayas at least, because if he was seen people would assume he was a Yeti. The ship said it would think about it (which meant No).

About the middle of June the ship suddenly asked me to go to Oslo for the day. Linter had asked to see me.

A module dropped me in woods near Sandvika in the bright, early morning. I caught a bus to the centre and walked up to the Frogner park. I found the bridge over the river which Linter wanted to use as a rendezvous, and sat on the parapet.

I didn't recognize him at first. I usually recognize people from the way they walk, and Linter's gait had altered. He looked thinner and more pale; not so physically imposing and immediate. Same suit as in Paris, though it looked baggier on him now, and slightly shabby. He stopped a metre away.

"Hello." I held out my hand. He shook it, nodded.

‹ "It's good to see you again. How are you keeping?" His voice was weaker sounding, less sure, somehow.

I shook my head, smiling. "Perfectly well, of course."

"Oh yes, of course." He was avoiding my eyes.

He made me feel a little awkward, just standing there, so I slid down off the parapet and stood in front of him. He seemed to be smaller than I remembered. He was rubbing his hands together as though it was cold, and looking up the broad avenue of bizarre Vigoland sculptures into the northern blue-morning sky. "Do you want to walk?" he asked.

"Yes, let's." We started across the bridge, towards the first flight of steps on the far side of the obelisk and fountain.

"Thank you for coming." Linter looked at me, then quickly away.

"That's all right. Pleasant city." I took off my leather jacket and slung it over my shoulder. I was wearing jeans and boots, but it was a blouse and skirt day really. "So, how are you getting on?"

"I'm still staying, if that's what you want to know." Defensively.

"I assumed you were."

He relaxed, coughed. We walked across the broad, empty bridge. It was still too early for most people to be up and about, and we seemed to be alone in the park. The severe, square, stone-plinthed lights of the bridge went slowly by, counterpoints to the curves of the strange statues.

"I...I wanted to give you this." Linter stopped, felt inside his jacket and brought out what looked like a gold-plated Parker pen. He twisted the top off; where the nib should have been there was a grey tube covered in tiny coloured symbols which belonged to no language on Earth. A little red tell-tale winked lazily. It looked insignificant, somehow. He put the top back on the terminal. "Will you take it?" he said, blinking.

"Yes, if you're sure."

"I haven't used it for weeks."

"How did you ask the ship to see me?"

"It sends down drones to talk to me. I offered the terminal to them, but they wouldn't take it. The ship won't take it. I don't think it wants to be responsible."

"You want me to be?"

"As a friend. I'd like you to; please. Please take it."

"Look, why not keep it but don't use it. In case there's some emergency—"

"No. No; just take it, please." Linter looked into my eyes for a moment. "It's just a formality."

I felt a strange urge to laugh, the way he said that. Instead I took the terminal from him and stuffed it into my bomber jacket. Linter sighed. We walked on.

It was a lovely day. The sky was cloudless, the air clear, and fragrant with mixtures of the sea and land. I wasn't sure whether there really was something about that quality of light that made it northern; perhaps it only looked different because you knew there was just a thousand kilometres or so of as clear, still fresher, colder air between you and the Arctic sea, the great bergs and the millions of square kilometres of ice and snow. It was like being on *another* planet.

We walked up the steps, Linter seeming to study each one. I was looking around, drinking in the sight and sound and smell of this place, reminding me of my holidays from London. I looked at the man by my side.

"You know you're not looking too well."

He didn't meet my gaze, but appeared to study some distant stonework at the end of the walk. "Well…no, I guess you could say I've changed." He smiled uncertainly. "I'm not the man I was."

Something about the way he said it made me shiver. He was watching his feet again.

"You staying here, in Oslo?" I asked him.

"For the moment, yes. I like it here. It doesn't feel like a capital city; clean and compact, but—" He broke off, shook his head at something. "I'll move on soon though, I think."

We went on, mounting the steps. Some of the Vigoland sculptures made me feel distinctly uncomfortable. A wave of something like revulsion swept over me, startling me; some planetary repugnance in this northern city. In this world now, they were talking of abandoning the B1 bomber to go ahead with the cruise missile. What had started out as the

Neutron Bomb had euphemized into the Enhanced Radiation Warhead and finally into the Reduced Blast Device.
They're all sick and so's he, I thought suddenly. Infected.
No, that was stupid. I was getting xenophobic. The fault was
within, not without.

"Do you mind if I tell you something?"

"What do you mean?" I said. What a weird thing to say, I
thought.

"Well you might find it...distasteful; I don't know."

"Tell me anyway. I have a strong constitution."

"I got...I asked the ship to ah...alter me." He looked at me
briefly. I inspected him. The slight stoop, the thinness and
paler skin wouldn't have required the services of the ship.
He saw me looking, shook his head. "No, nothing outside;
inside."

"Oh. What?"

"Well, I got it to...to give me a set of guts more like the locals.
And I had the drug glands taken out, and the uh—" he
laughed nervously "—the loop system in my balls."

I kept walking. I believed him, immediately. I couldn't believe
the ship had agreed to do it, but I believed Linter. I didn't
know what to say.

"So, I uh, don't have any choice about going to the toilet every
so often, and I...I had it work on my eyes, too." He paused.
Now it was my turn to keep looking at my feet, clomping
up the steps in my fancy Italian climbing boots. I didn't
think I wanted to hear this. "Sort of rewired so I see like
them. Bit fuzzier, sort of less...well, not fewer colours, but
more sort of...squashed up. Can't see much at night, either.
Same sort of thing on my ears and nose. But it...well it
almost enhances what you do experience, you know? I'm
still glad I had it done."

"Yeah." I nodded, not looking at him.

"My immune system isn't perfect anymore, either. I can get
colds, and...that sort of thing. I didn't get the shape of my
dick altered; decided it would pass. Did you know there

are considerable variations in genitalia here already? The Bushmen of the Kalahari have a permanent erection, and the women have the *Tablier Egyptien*; a small fold of flesh covering their genitals." He waved one hand. "So I'm not that much of a freak. I guess this isn't all that terrible really, is it? I don't know why I thought you might be disgusted or anything."

"Hmm." I was wondering what had possessed the ship to do all this to the man. It had agreed to carry out these... I could only think of them as mutilations...and yet it wouldn't accept his terminal. Why had it done this to him? It said it wanted him to change his mind, but it changed his body instead, pandering to his lunatic desire to become more like the locals.

"Can't change sex now, if I wanted to. Things'll still regrow if they get cut off; ship couldn't alter that, not quickly; take time; intensive care, and it wouldn't alter my...umm... clockspeed, what-d'you-call-it. So I'll still grow old slowly, and live longer than them...but I think it might relent later, when it knows I'm sincere."

All I could think of was that by converting Linter's physiology to a design closer to the planetary standard, the ship wanted to show the man what a nasty life they led. Perhaps it thought rubbing his nose in the Human Condition would send the man running back to the manifold delights of the ship, content with his Cultural lot at last.

"You don't mind, do you?"

"Mind? Why should I mind?" I said, and instantly felt foolish for sounding like something from a soap opera.

"Yes, I can see you do," Linter said. "You think I'm crazy, don't you?"

"All right." I stopped halfway up a flight of steps, turned to him. "I do, I think you're crazy to...to throw so much away. It's...it's wrong-headed of you, it's stupid. It's as if you're doing it just to annoy people, to test the ship. Are you trying to get it mad at you, or what?"

"Of course not, Sma." He looked hurt. "I don't care that much about the ship, but I was worried…I am concerned about what you might think." He took my free hand in both of his. They felt cold. "You're a friend. You matter to me. I don't want to offend anybody; not you, not anybody. But I have to do what feels right. This is very important to me; more important than anything else I've ever done before. I don't want to upset anybody, but…look, I'm sorry." He let go my hand.

"Yeah, I'm sorry too. But it's like mutilation. Like infection."

"Ah, we're the infection, Sma." He turned and sat down on the steps, looking back towards the city and the sea. "We're the ones who're different, we're the self-mutilated, the self-mutated. This is the mainstream; we're just like very smart kids; infants with a brilliant construction kit. They're real because they live the way they have to. We aren't because we live the way we want to."

"Linter," I said, sitting beside him. "This is the fucking mental home; the land of the midnight brain. This is the place that gave us Mutual Assured Destruction; they've thrown people into boiling water to cure diseases; they use Electro-Convulsive Therapy; a nation with a law against cruel and unusual punishments electrocutes people to death—"

"Go on; mention the death camps," Linter said, blinking at the blue distance.

"It was never Eden. It isn't ever going to be, but it might progress. You're turning your back on every advance we've made beyond where they are now, and you're insulting them as well as the Culture."

"Oh, pardon me." He rocked forward on his haunches, hugging himself.

"The only way they can go—and survive—is the same way we've come, and you're saying that's all shit. That's refugee mentality, and *they* wouldn't thank you for what you're doing. *They* would say you're crazy."

He shook his head, hands in his armpits, still staring away. "Maybe they don't have to take the same route. Maybe they don't need Minds, maybe they don't need more and more technology. They might be able to do it by themselves, without wars and revolutions even...just by understanding, by some...belief. By something more natural than we can understand. Naturalness is something they still understand."

"*Naturalness?*" I said, loudly. "This lot'll tell you *anything* is natural; they'll tell you greed and hate and jealousy and paranoia and unthinking religious awe and fear of God and hating anybody who's another colour or thinks different is *natural*. Hating blacks or hating whites or hating women or hating men or hating gays; that's *natural*. Dog-eat-dog, looking out for number one, no lame ducks...Shit, they're so convinced about what's natural it's the more sophisticated ones that'll tell you suffering and evil are natural and necessary because otherwise you can't have pleasure and goodness. They'll tell you any one of their rotten stupid systems is the natural and right one, the one true way; what's natural to them is whatever they can use to fight their own grimy corner and fuck everybody else. They're no more natural than us than an amoeba is more natural than them just because it's cruder."

"But Sma, they're living according to their instincts, or trying to. We're so proud of living according to our conscious belief, but we've lost the idea of shame. And we need that too. We need that even more than they do."

"*What?*" I shouted. I whirled round, took him by the shoulders and shook him. "We should be *what*? Ashamed of being conscious? Are you crazy? What's wrong with you? How can you *say* something like that?"

"Just listen! I don't mean they're better; I don't mean we should try to live like them, I mean that they have an idea of...of light and shade that we don't have. They're proud sometimes, too, but they're ashamed as well; they feel all-conquering and powerful but then they realize how powerless they really are. They know the good in them, but they know the evil in them, too; they recognize both, they *live* with both. We don't have that duality, that balance. And...and can't you see it might be more fulfilling for one individual—me— who *has* a Culture background who *is* aware of all life's possibilities, to live in this society, not the Culture?"

"So you find this...hellhole more fulfilling?"

"Yes, of course I do. Because there's—because it's just so... alive. In the end, they're right, Sma; it doesn't really matter that a lot of what's going on is what we—or even they— might call 'bad'; it's happening, it's there, and that's what matters, that's what makes it worthwhile to be here and be part of it."

I took my hands off his shoulders. "No. I don't understand you. Dammit Linter, you're more alien than they are. At least they have an excuse. God, you're the fucking mythical recent convert, aren't you? The fanatic. The zealot. I'm sorry for you, man."

"Well...thank you." He looked to the sky, blinking again. "I didn't want you to understand me too quickly, and—" he made a noise that was not quite a laugh "—I don't think you are, are you?"

"Don't give me that pleading look." I shook my head, but I couldn't stay angry with him looking like that. Something subsided in me, and I saw a sort of shy smile steal over Linter's face. "I am not," I said, "going to make this easy for you, Dervley. You're making a mistake. The biggest you'll ever make in your life. You'd better realize you're on your own. Don't think a few plumbing changes and a new set of bowel bacteria are going to make you any closer to *homo sapiens* either."

"You're a friend, Diziet. I'm glad you're concerned...but I think I know what I'm doing." ›

It was time for me to shake my head again, so I did. Linter held my hand while we walked back down to the bridge and then out of the park. I felt sorry for him because he seemed to have realized his own loneliness. We walked round the city for a while, then went to his apartment for lunch. His place was in a modern block down towards the harbour, not far from the massiveness of the city hall; a bare flat with white walls and little furniture. It hardly looked lived in at all save for a few late Lowry reproductions and sketches by Holbein.

It had clouded over in late morning. I left after lunch. I think he expected me to stay, but I only wanted to get back to the ship.

### 4.4: *God Told Me To Do It*

"Why did I do what?"

"What you did to Linter. Alter him. Revert him."

"Because he asked me to do it," the ship said. I was standing in the top hangar deck. I'd waited till I was back on the ship before I confronted it, via a remote drone.

"And of course it had nothing to do with hoping he might dislike the feeling so much he'd come back into the fold. Nothing to do with trying to shock him with the pain of being human when the locals have at least had the advantage of growing up with it and getting used to the idea. Nothing to do with letting him inflict a physical and mental torture on himself so you could sit back and say 'I told you so' after he came crying to you to take him back."

"Well as a matter of fact, no. You obviously believe I altered Linter for my own ends. That's not true. I did what I did because Linter requested it. Certainly I tried to talk him out of it, but when I was convinced that he meant what he said and he knew what he was doing and what it entailed—and when I couldn't reasonably decide he was mad—I did what he asked.

"It did occur to me he might not enjoy the feeling of being something close to human-basic, but I thought it was obvious from what he'd said when we were talking it over beforehand that he didn't expect to enjoy it. He knew it would be unpleasant, but he regarded it as a form of birth, or rebirth. I thought it unlikely he would be so unprepared for the experience, and so shocked by it, that he would want to be returned to his genofixed norm, and even less likely that he would go on from there to abandoning his idea of staying on Earth altogether.

"I'm a little disappointed in you, Sma. I thought you would understand me. One's object in trying to be scrupulously fair and even-handed is not to seek praise, I'm sure, but one would hope that having done something more honest than convenient, one's motives would not be questioned in such an overtly suspicious manner. I could have refused Linter's request; I could have claimed that I found the idea unpleasant and didn't want to have anything to do with it. I could have built a perfectly adequate defence on aesthetic distaste alone; but I didn't.

"Three reasons: One; I'd have been lying. I don't find Linter any more repellent or disgusting than I did before. What matters is his mind; his intellect and the state it's in. Physiological details are largely irrelevant. Certainly his body is less efficient than it was before; less sophisticated, less damage-resistant, less flexible over a given range of conditions than, say, yours... but he's living in the Twentieth Century West, and at a comparatively privileged economic level; he doesn't *have* to have brilliant reflexes or better night-sight than an owl. So his integrity as a conscious entity is less affected by all the alterations I've carried out on him than it already was by the very decision to stay on Earth in the first place.

"Two; if anything is going to convince Linter we're the good guys, it's being fair and reasonable even when he might not be being so. To turn on him because he's not doing just as I would like, or just as any of us might like, would be to force him further into the idea that Earth is his home, humanity his kin.

"Three;—and this would be sufficient reason by itself—what are we supposed to be about, Sma? What is the Culture? What do we believe in, even if it hardly ever is expressed, even if we are embarrassed about talking about it? Surely in freedom, more than anything else. A relativistic, changing sort of freedom, unbounded by laws or laid-down moral codes, but—in the end—just because it is so hard to pin down and express, a freedom of a far higher quality than anything to be found on any relevant scale on the planet beneath us at the moment.

"The same technological expertise, the same productive surplus which, in pervading our society, first allows us to be here at all and after that allows us the degree of choice we have over what happens to Earth, long ago also allowed us to live exactly as we wish to live, limited only by being expected to respect the same principle applied to others. And *that's* so basic that not only does every religion on Earth have some similar form of words in its literature, but almost every religion, philosophy or other belief system ever discovered anywhere else contains the same concept. It is the embedded achievement of that oft-expressed ideal that our society is—perversely—rather embarrassed about. We live with, use, simply *get on* with our freedom as much as the good people of Earth talk about it; and we talk about it as often as genuine examples of this shy concept can be found down there.

"Dervley Linter is as much a product of our society as I am, and as such, or at least until he can be proved to be in some real sense 'mad,' he's perfectly correct in expecting to have his wishes fulfilled. Indeed the very fact he asked for such an alteration—and accepted it from me—may prove his thinking is still more Culture- than Earth-influenced.

"In short, even if I had thought that I had sound tactical reasons for refusing his request, I'd have had just as difficult a job justifying such an action as I would have had I just snapped the guy off-planet the instant I realized what he was thinking. I can only be sure in myself that I am in the right in trying to get Linter to come back if I am positive that my own behaviour—as the most sophisticated entity involved—is beyond reproach, and in as close accord with the basic principles of our society as it is within my power to make it."

I looked at the drone's sensing band. I'd stood stock still during all this, unreacting. I sighed.

"Well," I said, "I don't know; that sounds almost...noble." I folded my arms. "Only trouble is, ship, that I can never tell when you're on the level and when you're talking just for the sake of it."

The unit stayed where it was for a couple of seconds, then turned and glided off, without saying another word.


*4.5: Credibility Problem*

The next time I saw Li, he was wearing a uniform just like Captain Kirk's in *Star Trek*.

"Well, what on earth," I laughed.

"Don't mock, alien," Li scowled.

I was reading *Faust* in German and watching two of my friends playing snooker. The gravity in the snooker room was a little less than standard, to make the balls roll right. I'd asked the ship (when it was still talking to me) why it hadn't reduced its internal G to Earth's average, as it had done with its day-night cycle. "Oh, it would have meant too much recalibration," the ship had said. "I couldn't be bothered." How's that for Godlike omnipotence?

"You won't have heard," Li said, sitting beside me, "having been on EVA, but I'm intending to become captain of this tub."

"Are you really? Well that's fascinating." I didn't ask him what or where the hell EVA was. "And how exactly do you propose attaining this elevated, not to say unlikely position?"

"I'm not sure yet," Li admitted, "but I think I have all the qualifications for the post."

"Consider the liminal cue given; I know you're going to—"

"Bravery, resourcefulness, intelligence, the ability to handle men—women—; a razor sharp wit and lightning fast reactions. Also loyalty and the ability to be ruthlessly objective when the safety of my ship and crew are at stake. Except, of course, when the safety of the Universe as we know it is at stake, in which case I would reluctantly have to consider making a brave and noble sacrifice. Naturally, should such a situation ever arise, I'd try to save the officers and crew who serve beneath me. I'd go down with the ship, of course."

"Of course. Well, that's—"

"Wait; there's another quality I haven't mentioned yet."

"Are there any left?"

"Certainly. Ambition."

"Silly of me. Of course."

"It will not have escaped your attention that until now nobody ever thought of wanting to become captain of the *Arb*."

"A perhaps understandable lapse." Jhavins, one of my friends, brought off a fine cut on the black ball, and I applauded. "Good shot."

Li prodded my shoulder. "Listen properly."

"I'm listening, I'm listening."

"The point is that my wanting to become captain, I mean even thinking of the idea, means that I *should be* the captain, understand?"

"Hmm." Jhavins was lining up an unlikely cannon on a distant red.

Li made an exasperated noise. "You're humouring me; I thought *you* at least would argue. You're just like everybody else."

"Ah," I said. Jhavins hit the red, but just left it hanging over the pocket. I looked at Li. "An argument? All right; you—anybody—taking command of the ship is like a flea taking over control of a human...maybe even like a bacteria in their saliva taking them over."

"But why should it command itself? We made it; it didn't make us."

"So? And anyway *we* didn't make it; other machines made it... and even they only started it off; it mostly made itself. But anyway, you'd have to go back...I don't know how many thousand generations of its ancestors before you found the last computer or spaceship built directly by any of our ancestors. Even if this mythical 'we' had built it, it's still zillions of times smarter than we are. Would you let an ant tell you what to do?"

"Bacterium? Flea? Ant? Make up your mind."

"Oh go away and de-scale a mountain or something, you silly man."

"But we started all this; if it hadn't been for us—"

"And who started us? Some glop of goo on another rock-ball? A super-nova? The big bang? What's *starting* something got to do with it?"

"You don't think I'm serious, do you?"

"More terminal than serious."

"You wait," Li said, standing up and wagging a finger at me. "I'll be captain one day. And you'll be sorry; I had you down tentatively as science officer, but now you'll be lucky to make nurse in the sickbay."

"Ah, away and piss on your dilithium crystals."

## 5. You Would If You Really Loved Me

*5.1: Sacrificial Victim*

I stayed on the ship for a few weeks after that. It started talking to me again after a couple of days. I forgot about Linter
for a while; everybody on the *Arbitrary* seemed to be talking
about new films or old films or books, or about what was
happening in Kampuchea, or about Lanyares Sodel, who
was off fighting with the Eritreans. Lanyares used to live
on a plate where he and some of his pals played games
of soldiers using live kinetic ammunition. I recalled hearing about this and being appalled; even with medical gear
standing by and a full supply of drug glands it sounded
slightly perverse, and when I'd found out they didn't have
anything to protect their heads, I'd decided these guys were
crazy. You could have your brains splattered over the landscape! You could *die*!
But they enjoyed the fear, I suppose. I'm told some people do.
Anyway, Lanyares told the ship he wanted to take part in
some real fighting. The ship tried to talk him out of it,
but failed, so sent him down to Ethiopia. It tracked him
by satellite and tailed him with scout missiles, ready to zap
him back to the ship if he was badly wounded. After some
badgering, and having obtained Lanyares's permission, the
ship put the view from the missiles trailing him onto an
accessible channel, so anybody could watch. I thought this
was in even more dubious taste.
It didn't last. After about ten days Lanyares got fed up because
there wasn't much happening and so he had himself taken

back up to the ship. He didn't mind the discomfort, he said, in fact it was almost pleasant in a masochistic sort of way, and certainly made shipboard life seem more attractive. But the rest had been so *boring*. Having a good ring-ding battle on a plate landscape designed for the purpose was much more fun. The ship told him he was silly and packed him back off to Rio de Janeiro to be a properly behaved culture-vulture again. Anyway, it could have sent him to Kampuchea, I suppose; altered him to make him look Cambodian and thrown him into the middle of the butchery of Year Zero. Somehow I don't think that was quite what Lanyares had been looking for though.

I travelled around more of Britain, East Germany and Austria when I wasn't on the *Arbitrary*. The ship tried me in Pretoria for a few days, but I really couldn't take it; perhaps if it had sent me there first I'd have been all right, but after nine months of Earth maybe even my Cultured nerves were getting frayed, and the land of Separate Development was just too much for me. I asked the ship about Linter a few times, but only received All-Purpose Non-Committal Reply Number 63a, or whatever, so after a bit I stopped asking.


"What is beauty?"

"Oh ship, really."

"No, I'm being serious. We have a disagreement here."

I stood in Frankfurt am Main, on a suspension footbridge over the river, talking to the ship via my terminal. One or two people looked at me as they walked by, but I wasn't in the mood to care.

"All right, then. Beauty is something that disappears when you try to define it."

"I don't think you really believe that. Be serious."

"Look ship, I already know what the disagreement is. I believe that there is something, however difficult to define, which is shared by everything beautiful and cannot be signified by any other single word without obscuring more than is made clear. You think that beauty lies in utility."

"Well, more or less."

"So where's Earth's utility?"

"Its utility lies in being a living machine. It forces people to act and react. At that it is close to the theoretical limits of efficiency for a non-conscious system."

"You sound like Linter. A living machine, indeed."

"Linter is not totally wrong, but he is like somebody who has found an injured bird and kept it past the time it is recovered, out of a protectiveness he would not like to admit is centred on himself, not the animal. Well, there may be nothing more we can do for Earth, and it's time to let go... in this case it's we who have to fly away, but you see what I mean."

"But you agree with Linter there is something beautiful about Earth, something aesthetically positive no Culture environment could match?"

"Yes, I do. Few things are all gain. All we have ever done is maximize what happens to be considered 'good' at any particular time. Despite what the locals may think, there is nothing intrinsically illogical or impossible about having a genuine, functioning Utopia, or removing badness without removing goodness, or pain without pleasure, or suffering without excitement... but on the other hand there is nothing to say that you can always fix things up just the way you want them without running up against the occasional problem. We have removed almost all the bad in our environment, but we have not quite kept all the good. Averaged out, we're still way ahead, but we do have to yield to humans in some fields, and in the end of course theirs is a more interesting environment. Naturally so."

"'May you live in interesting times.'"

"Quite."

"I can't agree. I can't see the utility or the beauty in that. All I'll give you is that it might be a relevant stage to go through."

"Might be the same thing. A slight time-problem perhaps. You just happen to be here, now."

"As are they all."

I turned round and looked at a few of the people walking by. The autumn sun was low in the sky, a vivid red disc, dusty and gaseous and the colour of blood, and rubbed into these well-fed Western faces in an image of a poison-price. I looked them in the eyes, but they looked away; I felt like taking them by the collar and shaking them, screaming at them, telling them what they were doing wrong, telling them what was happening; the plotting militaries, the commercial frauds, the smooth corporate and governmental lies, the holocaust taking place in Kampuchea...and telling them too what was possible, how close they were, what they could do if they just got their planetary act together... but what was the point? I stood and looked at them, and found myself—half involuntarily—glanding *slow*, so that suddenly they all seemed to be moving in slow-motion, trailing past as though they were actors in a movie, and seen on a dodgy print that kept varying between darkness and graininess. "What hope for these people, ship?" I heard myself murmur, voice slurred. It must have sounded like a squawk to anybody else. I turned away from them, looking down at the river.

"Their children's children will die before you even look old, Diziet. Their grandparents are younger than you are now... In your terms, there is no hope for them. In theirs, every hope."

"And we're going to use the poor bastards as a control group."

"We're probably just going to watch, yes."

"Sit back and do nothing."

"Watching is a form of doing. And, we aren't taking anything away from them. It'll be as if we were never here."

"Apart from Linter."

"Yes," sighed the ship. "Apart from Mr. Problem."

"Oh ship, can't we at least stop them on the brink? If they do press the button, couldn't we junk the missiles when they're in flight, once they've had their chance to do it their way and blown it...couldn't we come in then? It would have served its purpose as a control by then."

"Diziet, you know that's not true. We're talking about the next ten thousand years at least, not the lead time to the Third World War. Being able to stop it isn't the point; it's whether in the very long result it is the right thing to do."

"Great," I whispered to the swirling dark waters of the Main. "So how many infants have to grow up under the shadow of the mushroom cloud, and just possibly die screaming inside the radioactive rubble, just for us to be sure we're doing the right thing? How certain do we have to be? How long must we wait? How long must we make *them* wait? Who elected us God?"

"Diziet," the ship said, its voice sorrowful, "that question is being asked all the time, and put in as many different ways as we have the wit to devise...and that moral equation is being re-assessed every nano-second of every day of every year, and every time we find some place like Earth—no matter what way the decision goes—we come closer to knowing the truth. But we can never be absolutely certain. Absolute certainty isn't even a choice on the menu, most times." There was a pause. Footsteps came and went behind me on the bridge.

"Sma," the ship said finally, with a hint of what might have been frustration in its voice, "I'm the smartest thing for a hundred light years radius, and by a factor of about a million...but even I can't predict where a snooker ball's going to end up after more than six collisions."

I snorted, could almost have laughed.

"Well," the ship said, "I think you'd better be on your way now."

"Oh?"

"Yes. A passer-by has reported a woman on the bridge, talking to herself and looking at the water. A policeman is now on his way to investigate, probably already wondering how cold the water is, and so I think you should turn to your left and walk smartly away before he arrives."

"Right you are," I said. I shook my head as I walked off in the dusk light. "Funny old world, isn't it, ship?" I said, more to myself than to it.

The ship said nothing. The suspended bridge, big as it was, responded to my stepping feet, moving up and down at me like some monstrous and clumsy lover.


## 5.2: Not Wanted On Voyage

Back on the ship.

For a few hours the *Arbitrary* had left the world's snow-flakes unmolested, and gone collecting other samples at Li's request.

The first time Li saw me on the ship he'd come up to me and whispered, "Take him to see *The Man Who Fell To Earth*," and slunk off. The next time I saw him he claimed it was the first time and I must be hallucinating if I thought we'd met before. A fine way to greet a friend and admirer, claiming he'd been going about whispering cryptic messages…

So; one moonless, November night, darkside over the Tarim Basin…

Li was giving a dinner party.

He was still trying to become captain of the *Arbitrary*, but he seemed to have his ideas about rank and democracy mixed up, because he thought the best way to become "skipper" was to get us all to vote for him. So this was going to be a campaign dinner.

We sat in the lower hangar space, surrounded by our hardware. There were about two hundred people gathered in the hangar; everybody still on the ship was present, and many had come back off-planet just for the occasion. Li had us all sit ourselves round three giant tables, each two metres broad and at least ten times that in length. He'd insisted they should be proper tables, and complete with chairs and place settings and all the rest, and the ship had reluctantly filched a small Sequoia and done all the carving and turning and whatever to produce the tables and everything that went with them. To compensate, it had planted several hundred oaks in its upper hangar, using its own stored biomass as a growing medium; it would plant the saplings on Earth before it left.

When we were all seated, and had started talking amongst ourselves—I was sitting between Roghres and Ghemada— the lights around us dimmed, and a spotlight picked out Li, walking out of the darkness. We all sat back or craned forward, watching him.

There was much laughter. Li had greenish skin, pointed ears, and wore a *2001*-style spacesuit with a zig-zag silver flash added across the chest (held on by micro-rivets, he told me later). He sported a long red cape which flowed out behind from his shoulders. He held the suit helmet in the crook of his left arm. In his right hand he gripped a *Star Wars* light sword. Of course, the ship had made him a *real* one.

Li walked purposefully to the head of the middle table, tramped on an empty seat at its head and strode onto the table top, clumping down the brightly polished surface between the glittering place settings (the cutlery had been borrowed from a locked and forgotten storeroom in a palace on a lake in India; it hadn't been used for fifty years, and would be returned, cleaned, the next day...as would the dinner service itself, borrowed for the night from the Sultan of Brunei—without his permission), past the starched white napkins (from the *Titanic*; they'd be cleaned too and put back on the floor of the Atlantic), in the midst of the glittering glassware (Edinburgh Crystal, removed for a few hours from packing cases stowed deep in the hold of a freighter in the South China Sea, bound for Yokohama) and the candelabra (from a cache of loot lying under a lake near Kiev, sunk there by retreating Nazis judging from the sacks; also due to be replaced after their bizarre orbital excursion) until he stood in the centre of the middle table, maybe two metres from where I, Roghres and Ghemada sat.

"Ladies and gentlemen!" Li shouted, arms outstretched, helmet in one hand, sword humming brightly in the other. "The food of Earth! Eat!"

He assumed a dramatic pose, pointing the sword back up the table, gazing heroically along its green glowing length, and leaning forward, one knee bending. The ship either manipulated its gravity field or Li had an AG harness under the suit, because he rose silently from the table and drifted along above it (holding the pose) to the far end, where he dropped gracefully and sat in the seat he'd used earlier as a step. There was scattered applause and some hooting.

Meanwhile, dozens of drones and slaved trays had made their way out of the elevator shaft and approached the tables, bringing food.

We ate. It was all ethnic food, though not actually brought up from the planet; vat-grown ship food, though not a gourmet on Earth could have spotted any difference between our stuff and the real thing. From what I could see, Li had used the *Guinness Book of Records* as his wine list. The ship's copies of the wines involved were so good—we were told—that the ship itself couldn't have told them apart from the real thing.

We chomped and gurgled our way through an eclectic but relatively orthodox series of courses, chatting and fooling, and wondering whether Li had anything else planned; this all seemed disappointingly conventional. Li came round, asking how we were enjoying the meal, refilling our glasses, suggesting we try different dishes, saying he hoped he could count on our vote on election day, and sidestepping awkward questions about the Prime Directive.

Finally, much later, maybe a dozen courses later, when we were all sitting there bloated and content and mellow and sipping on our brandies and whiskies, we got Li's campaign speech...plus a dainty dish to set before the Culture.

I was a little drowsy. Li had come round with huge Havana cigars, and I'd taken one, and let the drug get to me. I was sitting there, puffing determinedly on the fat drug-stick, surrounded by a cloud of smoke, wondering what the natives saw in a tobacco high, but otherwise feeling just fine, when Li banged on the table with the pommel of the light sword and then climbed up and stood where his place setting had been (bang went one of the Sultan's plates, but I suspect the ship managed to repair it). The lights went out, leaving one spot on Li.

I used some *snap* to clear the sleepiness and stubbed the cigar out.

* "Ladies and gentlemen," Li said in a passable English, before continuing in Marain. "I have gathered you here this eve-ning to talk to you about Earth and what should be done with it. It is my hope and wish that after you've heard what I have to say you will agree with me on the only possible course of action...but first of all, let me say a few words about myself." There were jeers and cat-calls as Li bent and took up his glass of brandy. He drained the glass and threw it over his shoulder. A drone must have caught it in the shadows because I didn't hear it land.

"First of all," Li rubbed his chin, stroking the long hair. "Who am I?" He ignored a variety of shouts telling him "a total fucking idiot," and the like, and continued. "I am Grice-Thantapsa Li Brase 'ndane dam Sione; I am one hundred and seventeen years old, but wise beyond my years. I have been in Contact only six years, but I have experienced

---

* The following speech—sourced from the *Arbitrary*'s own files—has been rendered as accurately as possible. Mr. 'ndane's grammatical eccen-tricities are difficult to reproduce in English.—"The Drone"

much in that time, and so can speak with some author-
ity on Contact matters. I am the product of perhaps eight
thousand years of progress beyond the stage of the planet
that lies beneath our feet." (Cries of "Not much to show
for it, huh?," etc.) "I can track my ancestry back by name
for at least that amount of time, and if you went back to the
first dim glimmerings of sentience and you could end up
going back—" ("last week?" "your mother") "—through
tens of thousands of generations.

"My body is altered, of course; tuned to a high pitch of efficiency in terms of survivability and pleasure,—" ("don't worry,
it doesn't show") "—and just as I inherited that alteration, so
shall I pass it on to any children of my own." ("please, Li;
we've just eaten.") "We have remade ourselves just as we
have made our machines; we can fairly claim to be largely
our own work.

"However; in my head, literally inside my skull, in my brain, I
am potentially as stupid as the most recently born babe in
the most deprived area on Earth." He paused, smiling, to let
the cat-calls subside. "We are who we are as much because
of what we experience and are taught as we grow—the way
we are brought up, in other words—as we are because we
inherit the general appearance of pan-humanism, the more
particular traits associated with the Culture meta-species,
and the precise genetic mix contributed by our parents,
including all those wonderful tinkered-with bits." ("tinker
with your own bits, laddy.")

"So if I can claim to be morally superior to some denizen
of those depths of atmosphere beneath us, it is because
that is the way I was brought up. We are truly raised; they
are squashed, trimmed, trained, made into *bonsai*. Theirs
is a civilization of deprivation; ours of finely balanced
satisfaction ever teetering on the brink of excess. The
Culture could afford to let me be whatever it was within
my personal potential to become; so, for good or ill, I am
fulfilled.

"Consider; I think I can truthfully claim to be a more-or-less average Culture person, as can all of us here. Certainly, *we're* in Contact, so we might be a little more interested in travelling abroad and meeting people than the mean, but in general terms any one of us could be picked at random and represent the Culture quite adequately; the choice of who you would pick to represent Earth fairly I leave to your imagination.

"But back to me; I am as rich and as poor as anybody in the Culture (I use these words because it's to Earth I want to compare our present position). Rich; trapped as I am on board this uncaptained, leaderless tub, my wealth may not be very obvious, but it would seem immense to the average Earther. At home I have the run of a charming and beautiful Orbital which would seem very clean and uncrowded to somebody from Earth; I have unlimited access to the free, fast, safe and totally dependable underplate transport system; I live in a wing of a family home of mansion proportions surrounded by hectares of gorgeous gardens. I have an aircraft, a launch, the choice of mount from a large stable of *aphores*,* even the use of what would be called a spaceship by these people, plus a wide choice of deep space cruisers. As I say, I'm constrained at the moment by being in Contact, but of course I could leave at any moment, and within months be home, with another two hundred years or more of carefree life to look forward to; and all for nothing; I don't have to *do* anything for all this.

"But, at the same time, I am poor. I own nothing. Just as every atom in my body was once part of something else, in fact part of many different things, and just as the elementary particles were themselves part of other patterns before they came together to form the atoms that make up the magnificent physical and mental specimen you see standing

* I thought the phonetic equivalent was better than something strained like "horsoid."—"The Drone"

so impressively before you…yes, thank you…and just as one day every atom of my being will one day be part of something else—a star, initially, because that is the way we choose to bury our dead—again, so everything around me, from the food that I eat and the drink that I drink and the figurine that I carve and the house I inhabit and the clothes I wear so elegantly…to the module I ride to the Plate that I stand on and the star that warms me is there *when* I am there rather than *because* I am. These things may be arranged for me, but in that sense I only happen to be me, and they would be there for anybody else—should they desire them—too. I do not, emphatically *not* own them.

"Now, on Earth things are not quite the same. On Earth one of the things that a large proportion of the locals is most proud of is this wonderful economic system which, with a sureness and certainty so comprehensive one could almost imagine the process bears some relation to their limited and limiting notions of either thermodynamics or God, all food, comfort, energy, shelter, space, fuel and sustenance gravitates naturally and easily away from those who need it most and towards those who need it least. Indeed, those on the receiving end of such *largesse* are often harmed unto death by its arrival, though the effects may take years and generations to manifest themselves.

"To combat this insidious and disgusting travesty of sensible human relationships on a truly fundamental level was patently impossible on an infested dunghill like Earth, so deprived as it obviously was of meaningful genetic choice at a fundamental level and therefore philosophical options on a more accessible scale, and it became obvious—through the perverse logic inherent in the species and the process they had entailed—that the only way to react to such a system that had any chance of making it worse, and conditions that much less bearable, was to accept it on its own terms; go into competition with it!

"Now, quite apart from the fact that, from the point of view of the Earther, socialism suffers the devastating liability of only exhibiting internal contradictions when you are trying to use it as an adjunct to your own stupidity (unlike capitalism, which again, from the point of view of the Earther, happily has them built in from the start), it is the case that because Free Enterprise got there first and set up the house rules, it will always stay at least one kick ahead of its rivals. Thus, while it takes Soviet Russia a vast amount of time and hard work to produce one inspired lunatic like Lysenko, the West can so arrange things that even the dullest farmer can see it makes more sense to burn his grain, melt his butter and wash away the remains of his pulped vegetables with his tanks of unused wine than it does to actually sell the stuff to be consumed.

"And note that even if this mythical yokel did decide to sell the stuff, or even give it away—the Earthers have an even more devastating trick they can perform; they show you that those foods aren't even needed anyway! They wouldn't feed the least productive, most unimportant untouchable from Pradesh, tribesperson from Darfur or peon from Rio Branco! The Earth has more than enough to feed all its inhabitants every day *already*! A truth so seemingly world-shattering one wonders that the oppressed of Earth don't rise up in flames and anger yesterday! But they don't, because they are so infected with the myth of self-interested advancement, or the poison of religious acceptance, they either only want to make their own way up the pile so they can shit upon everybody else, or actually feel grateful for the attention when their so-called betters shit on them!

"It is my contention that this is either an example of the most formidable and blissfully arrogant use of power and existing advantage...or scarcely credible stupidity.

"Now then. Suppose we make ourselves known to this ghastly rabble; what happens?" Li stretched his arms out, and looked round us all just long enough to get a few people starting to answer him back, then roared on; "I'll tell you what! They won't believe us! Oh, so we have moving maps of the galaxy accurate to a millimetre contained in something the size of a sugar cube, oh so we can make Orbitals and Rings and get across the galaxy in a year and make bombs too small to see that could tear their planet apart…" Li sneered, let one hand flap limp. "Nothing. These people expect time travel, telepathy, matter transmission. Yes, we can say, 'Well, we do have a very limited form of prescience through the use of anti-matter at the boundary of the energy grid which lets us see nearly a milli-second into…' or 'Well, we usually train our minds in a way not entirely compatible with natural telepathic empathy, such as it is, but see this machine here…? Well, if you ask it nicely…' or 'Well, displacing isn't quite transmission of matter, but…'* They will laugh us out of the UN building; especially when they discover we haven't even got out of our home galaxy yet…unless you count the Clouds, but I doubt they would. And anyway; what is the Culture as a society compared to what they expect? They expect capitalists in space, or an empire. A libertarian-anarchist utopia? Equality? Liberty? Fraternity? This is not so much old-fashioned stuff as simply unfashionable stuff. Their warped minds have taken them away on an evaporatingly stupid side track off the main sequence of social evolution, and we are probably more alien than they are capable of understanding.

"So, the ship thinks we should just sit and *watch* this pack of genocidal buffoons for the next few millenia?" Li shook his head, wagged one finger. "I think not. I have a better idea, and I shall put it into effect as soon as I am elected captain. But now," he raised his hands and clapped. "The sweet course."

The drones and units reappeared, holding small steaming bowls of meat. Li topped up a few of the glasses nearest

* See; I told you.—"The Drone"

him and urged everybody else to refill their own as the final course was distributed. I'd just about filled myself up on the cheeses, but after Li's speech I seemed to have a bit more room. Still, I was glad my bowl was small. The aroma coming off the meat was quite pleasant, but I didn't think, somehow, it was an Earth dish.

"Meat as a *sweet* dish?" Roghres said, sniffing the gently steaming bowl. "Hmm; smells sweet, certainly."

"Shit," Tel Ghemada said prodding at her own bowl, "I know what this is…"

"Ladies and gentlemen," Li said, standing with a bowl in one hand and a silver fork in the other. "A little taste of Earth… no; more than that: a chance for you to participate in the rough and tumble of living on a squalid backwater planet without actually having to leave your seat or get your feet dirty." He stabbed a bit of the meat, put it in his mouth, chewed and swallowed. "Human flesh, ladies and gents; cooked muscle of *hom. sap*…as I suspect few of you might have guessed. A little on the sweet side for my palate, but quite acceptable. Eat up."

I shook my head. Roghres snorted. Tel put her spoon down. I sampled some of Li's unusual dish while he continued. "I had the ship take a few cells from a variety of people on Earth. Without their knowledge, of course." He waved the sword vaguely at the table behind us. "Most of you over there will be eating either Stewed Idi Amin or General Pinochet Chilli Con Carne; here in the centre we have a combination of General Stroessner Meat Balls and Richard Nixon Burgers. The rest of you have Ferdinand Marcos Sauté and Shah of Iran Kebabs. There are, in addition, scattered bowls of Fricaséed Kim Il Sung, Boiled General Videla, and Ian Smith in Black Bean Sauce…all done just right by the excellent—if leaderless—chef we have around us. Eat up! Eat up!"

We ate up, most of us quite amused. One or two thought the idea a little too outré, and some affected boredom because they thought Li needed discouragement not accomplices, while a few were just too full already. But the majority laughed and ate, comparing tastes and textures.

"If they could see us now," Roghres giggled. "Cannibals from outer space!"

When we were mostly done, Li stood on the table again and clapped his hands above his head. "Listen! Listen! Here's what I'll do if you make me captain!" The noise died away slowly, but there was still a fair amount of chattering and laughter. Li raised his voice. "Earth is a silly and boring planet. If not, then it is too deeply unpleasant to be allowed to exist! Dammit, there's something *wrong* with those people! They are beyond redemption and hope! They are *not* very bright, they are incredibly bigoted, and unbe-fucking-lievably cruel, both to their own kind and any other species that has the misfortune to stray within range, which of course these days means damn nearly every species; and they're slowly but determinedly fucking up the entire planet..." Li shrugged and looked momentarily defensive. "Not a particularly exciting or remarkable planet, for a life-sustainer type, true, but it's still a planet, it is quite pretty, and the principle remains. Frighteningly dumb or majestically evil, I suggest there is only one way to deal with this incontestably neurotic and clinically insane species, and that is to destroy the planet!"

Li looked round at this point, waiting to be interrupted, but nobody was rising to the bait. Those of us not distracted by the drink, whatever drugs, or each other, just sat smiling indulgently and waited to see what Li's next crazy idea was. He went on. "Now, I know this might seem a little extreme to some of you—" (cries of "no no," "bit lenient if you ask me," "wimp!" and "yeah; nuke the fuckers") "—and more importantly *very* messy, but I have talked it over with the ship, and it informs me that the best method from my point of view is actually quite elegant, as well as extremely effective.

"All we do is drop a micro black hole into the centre of the planet. Simple as that; no untidy debris left floating about, no big, vulgar flash, and, if we do it right, no upsetting the rest of the solar system. It takes longer than displacing a few tonnes of CAM into the core, but even that has the advantage of giving the humans time to reflect on their past follies, as their world is eaten away beneath them. In the end, all you'd have left is something about the size of a large pea in the same orbit as the Earth, and a minor amount of X-ray pollution from meteoric material. Even the moon could stay where it is. A rather unusual planetary sub-system, but—in terms of scale as much as anything else—a fitting monument, or memorial—" (Here Li smiled at me. I winked back.) "—to one of the more boringly inept rabbles marring the face of our fair galaxy.

"Couldn't we just wipe the place clear with a virus, I hear you ask? But no. While it is true that the humans have still done *relatively* little damage to their planet so far—from a distance it still looks fine—it is still the case that the place has been contaminated. Even if we wiped all human life off the rock-ball, people would still look down at the thing and shiver, recalling the pathetic but fiercely self-destructive monsters that once stalked its surface. However...even memories find it difficult to haunt a singularity."

Li stuck the point of the light sword into the top of the table and made to lean on the pommel; the wood flared and burned, and the sword started to drill through the flaming redwood in a cloud of smoke. Li pulled the sword out, shoved it in its scabbard and repeated the manoeuvre while somebody poured a small fortune in wine over the burning wood. ("Did they have scabbards?" Roghres asked, puzzled. "I thought they just turned it off...") The resulting steam and fumes rose dramatically around Li as he leant on the pommel of the sword and looked seriously and sincerely at all of us. "Ladies and gentlemen," he nodded, grim-faced. "This, I submit, is the only solution; a genocide to end all

genocides. We have to destroy the planet in order to save
it. Should you decide to do me the honour of electing me
as your ruler, to serve you, I shall set about putting this
plan into immediate effect, and shortly Earth, and all its
problems, will cease to exist. Thank you."
Li bowed, turned, stepped down and sat.
Those of us who'd still been listening clapped, and eventually
more or less everybody joined in. There were a few fairly
irrelevant questions about stuff like accretion disks, lunar
tidal forces, and conservation of angular momentum, but
after Li had done his best to answer those, Roghres, Tel,
Djibard and I went to the head of the table, lifted Li up,
carried him down the length of the table to the sound of
cheers, took him into the lower accommodation level, and
threw him in the pool. Fused the light sabre, but I don't
think the ship meant to leave Li with something that dangerous to wave around anyway.
We finished the fun off on a remote beach in Western Australia in the very early morning, swimming off our heavy
bellies and wine-fuddled heads in the slow rollers of the
Indian Ocean, or basking in the sunlight.
That's what I did; just lay there on the sand, listening to a still
pool-damp Li tell me what a great idea it was to blow the
entire planet away (or suck the entire planet away). I listened
to people splashing in the waves, and tried to ignore Li. I
dozed off, but I was woken up for a game of hide-and-seek
in the rocks, and later we sat around and had a light picnic.
Later, Li had us all play another game; guess the generalization.
We each had to think of one word to describe humanity;
Man, the species. Some people thought it was silly, just on
principle, but the majority joined in. There were sugges-
tions like "precocious," "doomed," "murderous," "inhuman," and "frightening." Most of us who'd been on-planet
must have been falling under the spell of humanity's own
propaganda, because we tended to come up with words
like "inquisitive," "ambitious," "aggressive," or "quick."

Li's own suggestion to describe humanity was "*MINE!*," but then somebody thought to ask the ship. It complained about being restricted to one word, then pretended to think for a long time, and finally came up with "gullible."

"Gullible?" I said.

"Yeah," said the remote drone. "Gullible...and bigoted."

"That's two words," Li told it.

"I'm a fucking starship; I'm allowed to cheat."

Well, it amused me. I lay back. The water sparkled, the sky seemed to ring with light, and way in the distance a black triangle or two carved the perimeter of the field the ship was laying down under the chopping blue sea.

## 6: Undesirable Alien

*6.1: You'll Thank Me Later*

December. We were finishing off, tying up the loose ends.
There was an air of weariness about the ship. People
seemed quieter. I don't think it was just tiredness. I think
it was more likely the effect of a realized objectivity, a dis-
tancing; we had been there long enough to get over the ini-
tial buzz, the honeymoon of novelty and delight. We were
starting to see Earth as a whole, not just a job to be done
and a playground to explore, and in looking at it that way,
it became both less immediate and more impressive; part
of the literature, something fixed by fact and reference, no
longer ours; a droplet of knowledge already being absorbed
within the swelling ocean of the Culture's experience.
Even Li had quieted down. He held his elections, but only a
few people were indulgent enough to vote, and we just did
it to humour him. Disappointed, Li declared himself the
ship's captain in exile (no, I never understood that either),
and left it at that. He took to betting against the ship on
horse races, ball games and football matches. The ship must
have been fixing the odds, because it ended up owing Li a
ridiculous amount of money. Li insisted on being paid so
the ship fashioned him a flawless cut diamond the size of
his fist. It was his, the ship told him. A gift; he could *own* it.
(Li lost interest in it after that though, and tended to leave
it lying around the social spaces; I stubbed a toe on it at
least twice. In the end he got the ship to leave the stone in
orbit around Neptune on our way out of the system; a joke.)

I spent a lot of time on the ship playing *Tsartas* music, though more to compose myself than anything else.*

I had my Grand Tour, like most of the others on the ship, so spent a day or so in all the places I wanted to see; I saw sunrise from the top of Khufu and sunset from Ayers Rock. I watched a pride of lions laze and play in Ngorongoro, and the tabular bergs calve from the Ross ice shelf; I watched condors in the Andes, musk ox on the tundra, polar bears on the Arctic ice and jaguars slinking through the jungle. I skated on Lake Baikal, dived over the Great Barrier Reef, strolled along the Great Wall, rowed across Dal and Titicaca, climbed Mount Fuji, took a mule down the Grand Canyon, swam with the whales off Baja California, and hired a gondola to cruise round Venice, through the cold mists of winter under a sky that to me looked old and tired and worn.

I know some people did go to the ruins at Angkor, safety guaranteed by the ship, its drones and knife missiles...but not I. No more could I visit the Potala, however much I wanted to.

We were due for a couple of months R&R on an Orbital in Trohoase cluster; standard procedure after immersion in a place like Earth. Certainly, I wasn't in the mood for any more exploring for a while; I was drained, sleeping five or six hours a night and dreaming heavily, as though the pressure of artificially crammed information I'd started out with as briefing—combined with everything I'd experienced personally—was too much for my poor head, and it was leaking out when my guard was down.

I'd given up on the ship. Earth was going to be a Control; I'd failed. Even the fall-back position, of waiting until Armageddon, was disallowed. I argued it out with the ship in a crew assembly, but couldn't even carry the human vote with me. The *Arbitrary* copied to the *Bad For Business* and the

* Sma uses a relatively equivalent play on words here.—"The Drone"

rest, but I think it was just being kind; nothing I said made any difference. So I made music, took my Grand Tour, and slept a lot.

I finished my Tour, and said goodbye to Earth, on the cliffs of a chilly, wind-swept Thíra, looking out over the shattered caldera to where the ruby-red sun met the Mediterranean; a livid plasma island sinking in the wine-dark sea. Cried.

So I wasn't at all pleased when the ship asked me to hit dirt for one last time.

"But I don't want to."

"Well, that's all right, if you're quite sure. I'm not asking you to do it for your own good, I must admit, but I did promise Linter I'd ask, and he did seem quite anxious to see you before we left."

"Oh...but *why*? What does he want from me?"

"He wouldn't say. I didn't talk to him all that long. I sent a drone down to tell him we were leaving soon, and he said he would only talk to you. I told him I'd ask but I couldn't guarantee anything...he was adamant though; only you. He won't talk to me. Oh well. Such is life. Not to worry. I'll tell him you won't—" the small unit started to drift away, but I pulled it back.

"No; no, stop; I'll go. God dammit, I'll go. Where? Where does he want to meet?"

"New York City."

"Oh no," I groaned.

"Hey, it's an interesting place. You might like it."


*6.2: The Precise Nature Of The Catastrophe*

A General Contact Unit is a machine. In Contact you live inside one, or several, plus a variety of Systems Vehicles, for most of your average thirty-year stint. I was just over halfway through my spell and I'd been on three GCUs;

the *Arbitrary* had been my home for only a year before we found Earth, but the craft before it had been an Escarpment class too. So I was used to living in a device...nevertheless; I'd never felt so machine-trapped, so tangled and caught and snarled up as I did after an hour in the Big Apple.

I don't know if it was the traffic, the noise, the crowds, the soaring buildings or the starkly geometric expanses of streets and avenues (I mean, I've never even *heard* of a GSV which laid out its accommodation as regularly as Manhattan), or just everything together, but whatever it was, I didn't like it. So; a bitterly cold, windy Saturday night in the big city on the Eastern seaboard, only a couple of weeks' shopping left till Christmas, and me sitting in a little coffee shop on 42nd Street at eleven o'clock, waiting for the movies to end.

What was Linter playing at? Going to see *Close Encounters* for the seventh time, indeed. I looked at my watch, drank my coffee, paid the check and left. I tightened the heavy wool coat about me, pulled on gloves and a hat. I wore needlecords and knee-length leather boots. I looked around as I walked, a chill wind against my face.

What really got to me was the predictability. It *was* like a jungle. Oslo a rock garden? Paris a parterre, with its follies, shady areas and breeze-block garages inset? London with that vaguely conservatory air, a badly kept museum haphazardly modernized? Wien a too severe version of Paris, high starch collared, and Berlin a long garden party in the ruins of a baroque sepulchre? Then New York a rainforest; an infested, towering, teeming jungle, full of great columns that scratched at the clouds but which stood with their feet in the rot, decay and swarming life beneath; steel on rock, glass blocking the sun; the ship's living machine incarnate.

I walked through the streets, dazzled and frightened. The *Arbitrary* was just a tap on my terminal away, ready to send help or bounce me up on an emergency displace, but I still felt scared. I'd never been in such an intimidating place. I walked up 42nd Street and carefully crossed Sixth Avenue to walk along its far side towards the movie theatre.

People streamed out, talking in twos and groups, putting up collars, walking off quickly with their arms round each other to find someplace warm, or standing looking for a cab. Their breath misted the air in front of them, and from the lights of the mothership to the lights of the foyer to the lights of the snarling traffic they moved. Linter was one of the last out, looking thinner and paler than he had in Oslo, but brighter, quicker. He waved and came over to me. He buttoned up a fawn-coloured coat, then put his lips to my cheek as he reached for his gloves.

"Mmm. Hello. You're cold. Eaten yet? I'm hungry. Want to eat?"

"Hello. I'm not cold. I'm not hungry either, but I'll come and watch you. How are you?"

"Fine. Fine," he smiled.

He didn't look fine. He looked better than I remembered, but in big city terms, he was a bit scruffy and not very well-fed looking. That fast, edgy, high-pressure urban life had infected him, I guess.

He pulled on my arm. "Come on; let's walk. I want to talk."

"All right." We started along the sidewalk. Bustle-hustle, all their signs and lights and racket and smell, the white noise of their existence, a focus of all the world's business. How could they stand it? The bag ladies; the obvious loonies, eyes staring; the grotesquely obese; the cold vomit in the alleys and the bloodstains on the kerb; and all their signs, those slogans and lights and pictures, flickering and bright, entreating and ordering, enticing and demanding in a grammar of glowing gas and incandescing wire.

This was the soul of the machine, the ethological epicentre, the planetary ground zero of their commercial energy. I could almost feel it, shivering down like bomb-blasted rivers of glass from these undreaming towers of dark and light invading the snow-dark sky.

Peace in the Middle East? the papers asked. Better celebrate
Bokassa's coronation instead; better footage.

"You got a terminal?" Linter said. He sounded eager somehow.
"Of course."

"Turn it off?" he said. His eyebrows rose. He looked like a child
all of a sudden. "Please. I don't want the ship to overhear."

I wanted to say something to the effect that the ship could
have bugged every individual hair on his head, but didn't.
I turned the terminal brooch to standby.

"You seen *Close Encounters*?" Linter said, leaning towards me.
We were heading in the direction of Broadway.

I nodded. "Ship showed us it being made. We saw the final
print before anybody."

"Oh yes, of course." People bumped into us, swaddled in their
heavy clothes, insulated. "The ship said you're leaving soon.
Are you glad to be going?"

"Yes, I am. I didn't think I'd be, but I am. And you? Are you
glad to be staying?"

"Pardon?" A police car charged past, then another, sirens
whooping. I repeated what I'd said. Linter nodded and
smiled at me. I thought his breath smelled. "Oh yes," he
nodded. "Of course."

"I still think you're a fool, you know. You'll be sorry."

"Oh no, I don't think so." He sounded confident, not looking
at me, head held high as we walked down the street. "I don't
think so at all. I think I'm going to be very happy here."

Happy here. In the grand, cold design and the fake warmth of
the neon, while the drunks brown-bagged and the addicts
begged and the deadbeats searched for warmer gratings
and a thicker cardboard box. It seemed worse here; you
saw the same thing in Paris and London, but it seemed
worse here. Take a step from a shop you had to have an
appointment for, swathed in loot across the sidewalk to
the Roller, Merc or Caddy purring at the kerb, while some
poor fucked-up husk of a human lay just a spit away, but
you'd never notice them noticing...Or maybe I was just

too sensitive, shell-shocked; life really was a struggle on Earth, and the Culture's 100 per cent non-com. A year was as much as you could have expected any of us to handle, and I was near the end of my resistance.

"It'll all work out, Sma. I'm very confident."

Fall in the street here and they just walk around you...

"Yes, yes. I'm sure you're right."

"Look." He stopped, turned me by the elbow so that we stood face to face. "I'm going to have to tell you. I know you probably won't like me for it, but it's important to me." I watched his eyes, shifting to look at each of mine in turn. His skin looked more mottled than I remembered; some pore-deep dirt.

"What?"

"I'm studying. I'm going to enter the Roman Catholic Church. I've found Jesus, Diziet; I'm saved. Can you understand that? Are you angry with me? Does it upset you?"

"No, I'm not angry," I said flatly. "That's great, Dervley. If you're happy, I'm happy for you. Congratulations."

"That's great!" He hugged me. I was pressed against his chest; held; released. We resumed our walk, walking faster. He seemed pleased. "Damn, I can't tell you Dizzy; it's just so good to be here, to be alive and know there are so many people, so much happening! I wake up in the morning and I have to lie for a while just convincing myself I'm really here and it's all really happening to me; I really do. I walk down the street and I look at the people; just look at them! A woman was killed in the place I stay in last week; can you imagine that? Nobody heard a thing. I go out and I go on buses and I buy papers and watch old movies in the afternoon. Yesterday I watched a man being talked down from the Queensboro bridge. I think people were disappointed. D'you know, when he came down he tried to claim he was a painter?" Linter shook his head, grinning. "Hey, I read a terrible thing yesterday, you know? I read that there are times when there's a really complicated birth and the baby's caught inside the mother and probably already dead, and the doctor has to reach up inside the woman and take the baby's skull in his hand and crush it so they can save the mother. Isn't that terrible? I don't think I could have condoned that even before I found Jesus."

"Why couldn't they have done a Caesarean?"

"I don't know. I don't know. I wondered about that myself. You know I was thinking about coming up to the ship?" He looked briefly at me, nodded. "To see if anybody else might want to stay. I thought others might want to follow my example, especially after I'd talked to them, had a chance to explain. I thought they might see I was right."

"Why didn't you?" We stopped at another intersection. All the people charged around us, hurrying through the smells of burning petrol and cooking and rotten food. I smelled gas, and sometimes steam wrapped itself around us, damp and fragrant.

"Why didn't I?" Linter mused, watching the DON'T WALK sign. "I didn't think it would do any good. And I was afraid the ship might find a way of keeping me on board. Do you think I was foolish?"

I looked at him, while the steam curled round us and the sign changed to WALK, but I didn't say anything. An old guy came up to us on the far sidewalk and Linter gave him a quarter.

"But I'll be fine by myself anyway." We turned down Broadway, heading towards Madison Square, past shops and offices, theatres and hotels, bars and restaurants and apartment blocks. Linter put his arm round my waist, squeezed me. "Come on, Dizzy, you aren't saying much."

"No, I'm not, am I?"

"I guess you still think I'm being stupid."

"No more than the locals."

He smiled. "They're really good people. What you don't understand is you have to translate behaviour as well as language. Once you do realize that you'll come to love these people the way I do. Sometimes I think they've come to terms with their technology better than we have, you know that?"

"No." No I didn't know that, here in mincerville, meat-grinder city. Come to terms with it; yeah sure…turn off the aiming computer, Luke; play the five tones; close your eyes and concentrate together, that's the way…nobody here but us Clears…hand me down that orgone box…

"I'm not getting through to you, Dizzy, am I? You're all closed up, not really here. You're halfway out the system already, aren't you?"

"I'm just tired," I told him. "Keep talking." I felt like a helpless, twitching, pink-eyed rat caught in a maze in some shining alien laboratory; vast and glittering with some lethal, inhuman purpose.

"They do so well, considering. I know there's a lot of horrible things going on, but it only seems so terrible because we pay so much attention to it. The vast majority of good stuff isn't newsworthy; we don't notice it. We don't see what a *good* time most of these people are having. I've met a lot of quite happy people, you know; I have friends. I met them through my work."

"You work?" I was actually interested.

"Ha ha. I thought the ship might not have told you that. Yes, I've had a job for the last couple of months; document translator for a big firm of lawyers."

"Uh-huh."

"What was I saying? Oh yeah; lots of people have a quite acceptable life; they're pretty comfortable in fact. People can have neat apartments, cars, holidays…and people can have children. *That's* a good thing, you know; you see a lot more children on a planet like this. I like children. Don't you?"

"Yes. I thought everybody did."

"Ha, well…anyway…in some ways these people would consider us backward, you know that? I know it might sound dumb, but it isn't. Look at transport; the aircraft I had on my home plate was on its third or fourth generation, nearly a thousand years old! These people change their automobiles every year! They have throwaway containers and disposable clothes and fashions that mean changing your clothes every year, every season!—"

"Dervley—"

"Compared to them, the Culture moves at a snail's pace!"

"Dervley, what was it you wanted to talk about?"

"Huh? Talk about?" Linter looked confused. We turned left onto Fifth Avenue. "Oh, nothing in particular, I guess. I just thought it'd be nice to see you before you left; wish you *bon voyage*. I hope you don't mind. You don't mind, do you? The ship said you might not want to come, but you don't mind, do you?"

"No, I don't mind."

"Good. Good, I didn't think…" His voice trailed off. We walked on in our own silence, in the midst of the city's continuous coughing and spitting and wheezing.

I wanted to go. I wanted to get out of this city and off this continent and up from this planet and onto the ship and out of this system…but something kept me walking with him, walking and stopping, stepping down and out, across and up, like another obedient part of the machine, designed to move, to function, to keep going regardless, to keep pressing on and plugging away, warming up or falling down but always always moving, down to the drug store or up to company president or just to stay a moving target, hugging the rails on a course you hardly needed to see so could stay blinkered on, missing the fallers and the lame around you and the trampled ones behind. Perhaps he was right and any one of us could stay here with him, just vanish into the city-space and disappear forever and never be thought of again, never think again, just obey orders and ordinances and do what the place demands, start falling and never stop, never find any other purchase, and our twistings and turnings and writhings as we fall, exactly what the city expects, just what the doctor ordered…

Linter stopped. He was looking through an iron grille at a shop selling religious statues, holy water containers, Bibles and commentaries, crosses and rosaries and crib and manger scenes. He stared down at it all, and I watched him. He nodded at the window display. "That's what we've lost, you know. What *you've* lost; all of you. A sense of wonder and awe and...sin. These people know there are still things they don't know, things that can still go wrong, things they can still do wrong. They still have the hope because the possibility is there. Without the possibility of failure, you can't have hope. They have hope. The Culture has statistics. We—it; the Culture—is too certain, too organized and stifled. We've choked the life out of life; nothing's left to chance. Take the chance of things going wrong out of life and it stops being life, don't you see?" His pinched, dark-browed face looked frustrated.

"No, I don't see," I told him.

He ran one hand through his hair, shook his head. "Look; let's eat, huh? I'm really hungry."

"OK; lead on. Where?"

"This way; somewhere really special." We started off in the same direction again, came to the corner of 48th Street and turned up that. A cold wind blew around us, scattering papers. "What I mean is, you have to have that potential for wrongness there or you can't live...or you can but it doesn't *mean* anything. You can't have the peak without the trough, or light without shade...it's not that you must have evil to have good, but you must have the possibility for evil. That's what the Church teaches, you know. That's the choice that Man has; he can choose to be good or evil; God doesn't force him to be evil any more than He forces him to be good. The choice is left to Man now as it was to Adam. Only in God is there any real chance of understanding and appreciating Free Will."

He pushed my elbow, steering me down an alley. A white and red sign glowed at the far end. I could smell food.

"You have to see that. The Culture gives us so much, but in fact it's only taking things away from us, lobotomizing everybody in it, taking away their choices, their potential for being really good or even slightly bad. But God, who is in all of us; yes, in you too, Diziet...perhaps even in the ship for all I know...God, who sees and knows all, who is all-powerful, all-knowing, in a way that no ship, no mere Mind can ever be; *infinitely* knowing, still allows us; poor, pathetic, fallible humanity—and by extension, pan-humanity...allows even us; the, the—"

It was dark in the alley, but I should still have seen them. I wasn't even listening properly to Linter, I was just letting him witter on, not concentrating. So I should have seen them, but I didn't, not until it was too late.

They moved out from behind us, knocking over a dustcan, shouting, crashing into us. Linter spun around, letting go of my elbow, I turned quickly. Linter held up one hand and said—did not shout—something I didn't catch. A figure rushed at me, half crouched. Somehow, without seeing it, I knew there was a knife.

It all remains so clear, so measured. I suppose some secretion had taken over the instant my midbrain realized what was happening. It seemed very light in the alley, and everybody else was moving slowly, along lines like laser beams or cross-hairs, casting weighted shadows in front of them along those lines in the direction they were moving.

I stepped to one side, letting the boy and the knife spin past. A right-foot trip and a little pressure on his wrist as he went by and he had to let the knife go. He stumbled and fell. I had the knife, and threw it far away down the alley before turning back to Linter.

Two of them had him on the ground, kicking and struggling. I heard him cry out once as I moved towards them, but I recall no other sound. Whether it was really as silent as I remember it, or whether I was simply concentrating on the sense that yielded the most information, I don't know. I caught the heels of one of them, and pulled, heaving him out and up, cracking his face against one boot where I'd stuck it out to meet him. I threw him out of the way. The other one was already up. Lines seemed to be bunching up at the side of my vision, and throbbing, making me think about how much time the first one had had to regain his balance if not his knife. I realized I wasn't doing this the way you were meant to. The one in front of me lunged. I stepped out of the way, turning again. I hit him on the head while I looked back at the first one, who was on his feet, coming forward, but hesitating at the side of the one I'd hit second, who was struggling up against the wall, holding his face; dark blood on pale skin.

They ran, as one, like a school of fish turning.

Linter was staggering, trying to stand. I caught him and he clutched at me, gripping my arm tightly, breath wheezing. He stumbled and sagged as we got to the red and white light outside the little restaurant. A man with a napkin stuffed in the top of his vest opened the door and looked out at us.

Linter fell at the doorstep. It was only then I thought of the terminal, and realized that Linter was gripping the top of my coat, where the terminal brooch was. The smells of cooking came out of the open door. The man with the napkin looked cautiously up and down the alley. I tried to prise Linter's fingers free.

"No," he said. "No."

"Dervley, let go. Let me get the ship."

"No." He shook his head. There was sweat on his brow, blood on his lips. A huge dark stain was spreading over the fawn coat. "Let me."

"What?"

"Lady?"

"No. Don't."

"Lady? Want me to call the cops?"

"Linter? Linter?"

"Lady?"

"*Linter!*"

When his eyes closed his grip loosened.

There were more people at the restaurant door. Somebody said, "Jesus." I stayed there, kneeling on the cold ground with Linter's face close to mine, thinking: How many films? (The guns quieten, the battle stops.) How often do they do this, in their commercial dreams? (Look after Karen for me... that's an order, mister... you know I always loved you... Killing of Georgie... Ici resté un deporté inconnu...) What am I doing here? Come on lady.

"Come on, lady. Come on, lady..." Somebody tried to lift me.

Then he was lying beside Linter looking hurt and surprised and somebody was screaming and people were backing off.

I started running. I jabbed the terminal brooch and shouted.

I stopped at the far end of the alley, near the street, and rested against a wall, looking at the dark bricks opposite.

A noise like a pop, and a drone sinking slowly down in front of me; a business-like black-body drone, the inky lengths of two knife missiles hovering on either side above eye level, twitchy for action.

I took a deep breath. "There's been a slight accident," I said calmly.

### 6.3: Halation Effect

I looked at Earth. It was shown, in-holo'd, on one wall of my cabin; brilliant and blue, solid and white-whorled.

"Then it was more like suicide," Tagm said, stretching out on my bed. "I didn't think Catholics—"

"But I cooperated," I said, still pacing up and down. "I let him do it. I could have called the ship. After he lost consciousness there was time; we could still have saved him."

"But he'd been altered back, Dizzy, and they're dead when their heart stops, aren't they?"

"No; there's two or three minutes after the heart stops. It was
enough time. I had enough time."

"Well then so did the ship. It *must* have been watching; it was
bound to have had a missile on the case." Tagm snorted.
"Linter was probably the most over-observed man on the
planet. The ship must have known too; it could have done
something. The ship had the control, it had the real-time
grasp; it isn't your responsibility, Dizzy."

I wished I could accept Tagm's moral subtraction. I sat down
on the end of the bed, head in my hands, staring at the
holo of the planet in the wall. Tagm came over, hugged me,
hands on my shoulders, head on mine. "Dizzy; you have to
stop thinking about it. Let's go do something. You can't sit
watching that damn holo all day."

I stroked one of Tagm's hands, gazed again at the slowly
revolving planet, my gaze flicking in one glance from pole to
equator. "You know, when I was in Paris, seeing Linter for
the first time, I was standing at the top of some steps in the
courtyard where Linter's place was, and I looked across it and
there was a little notice on the wall saying it was forbidden
to take photographs of the courtyard without the man's permission." I turned to Tagm. "They want to own the light!"

## 6.4: *Dramatic Exit*, Or, *Thank You And Goodnight*

At five minutes and three seconds past three AM, GMT, on
the morning of January the second, 1978, the General Contact Unit *Arbitrary* broke orbit above the planet Earth. It
left behind an octet of Main Observation Satellites—six of
them in near-GS orbits—a scattering of drones and minor
missiles, and a small plantation of young oaks on a bluff
near Elk Creek, California.

The ship had brought Linter's body back up, displacing it from
its freezer in a New York City morgue. But when we left,
Linter stayed, in a fashion. I argued he ought to be buried

on-planet, but the ship disagreed. Linter's last instructions regarding the disposal of his remains had been issued fifteen years earlier, when he first joined Contact, and were quite conventional; his corpse was to be displaced into the centre of the nearest star. So the sun gained a bodyweight, courtesy of Culture tradition, and in a million years, maybe, a little of the light from Linter's body would shine upon the planet he had loved.

The *Arbitrary* held its darkfield for a few minutes, then dropped it just past Mars (so there was just a chance it left an image on an Earth telescope). Meanwhile it was snapping all its various remote drones and sats away from the other planets in the system. It stayed in real space right up till the last moment (making it possible that its rapidly increasing mass produced a blip on a terrestrial gravity-wave experiment, deep in some mountain-mine), then totalled as it dispatched Linter's body into the stellar core, sucked a last few drones of Pluto and a couple of outlying comets, and slung Li's diamond at Neptune (where it's probably still in orbit).

I'd decided to leave the *Arbitrary* after the R&R, but after I'd relaxed on Svanrayt Orbital for a few weeks I changed my mind. I had too many friends on the ship, and anyway it seemed genuinely upset when it found out I was thinking of transferring. It charmed me into staying. But it never did tell me whether it had been watching Linter and me that night in New York.

So, did I really believe I was to blame, or was I kidding even myself? I don't know. I didn't know then, and I don't know now.

There was guilt, I recall, but it was an odd sort of guilt. What really annoyed me, what I did find hard to take, was my complicity not in what Linter was trying to do, and not in his own half-willed death, but in the generality of transferred myth those people accepted as reality.

It strikes me that although we occasionally carp about Having To Suffer, and moan about never producing *real* Art, and become despondent or try too hard to compensate, we are indulging in our usual trick of synthesizing something to worry about, and should really be thanking ourselves that we live the life we do. We may think ourselves parasites, complain about Mind-generated tales, and long for "genuine" feelings, "real" emotion, but we are missing the point, and indeed making a work of art ourselves in imagining such an uncomplicated existence is even possible. We have the best of it. The alternative is something like Earth, where as much as they suffer, for all that they burn with pain and confused, bewildered *angst*, they produce more dross than anything else; soap operas and quiz programmes, junk papers and pulp romances.

Worse than that, there is an osmosis from fiction to reality, a constant contamination which distorts the truth behind both and fuzzes the telling distinctions in life itself, categorizing real situations and feelings by a set of rules largely culled from the most hoary fictional clichés, the most familiar and received nonsense. Hence the soap operas, and those who try to live their lives as soap operas, while believing the stories to be true; hence the quizzes where the ideal is to think as close to the mean as possible, and the one who conforms utterly is the one who stands above the rest; the Winner...

They always had too many stories, I believe; they were too free with their acclaim and their loyalty, too easily impressed by simple strength or a cunning word. They worshipped at too many altars.

Well, there's your story.

Perhaps it's as well I haven't changed very much over the years; I doubt that it's much different from what I'd have written a year or a decade later, rather than a century.*

It's funny the images that stay with you though. Over the years one thing has haunted me, one dream recurred. It

* Ha!—"The Drone"

really has nothing to do with me in a sense, because it was something I never saw...yet it stays there, nevertheless.

I didn't want to be displaced, that night, nor did I want to travel out to somewhere remote enough for a module to pick me up without being seen. I got the black-body drone to lift me from the city; right up, darkfielded, into the sky in the midst of Manhattan, rising above all that light and noise into the darkness, quiet as any falling feather. I sat on the Drone's back, still in shock I suppose, and don't even remember transferring to the dark module a few kilometres above the grid of urban light. I saw but didn't watch, and thought not of my own flight, but about the other drones the ship might be using on the planet at the time; where they might be, what doing.

I mentioned the *Arbitrary* collected snowflakes. Actually it was searching for a pair of identical ice crystals. It had—has— a collection; not holes or figure break-downs, but actual samples of ice crystals from every part of the galaxy it has ever visited where it found frozen water. It only ever collects a few flakes each time, of course; a saturation pick-up would be...inelegant.

I suppose it must still be looking. What it will do if it ever does find two identical crystals, it has never said. I don't know that it really wants to find them, anyway.

But I thought of that, as I left the glittering, grumbling city beneath me. I thought—and I still dream about this, maybe once or twice a year—of some drone, its flat back star-dappled, quietly in the steppes or at the edge of a polynya off Antarctica, gently lifting a single flake of snow, teasing it away from the rest, and hesitating perhaps, before going, displaced or rising, taking its tiny, perfect cargo to the orbiting starship, and leaving the frozen plains, or the waste of ice, once more at peace.

## 7: Perfidy, *Or,* A Few Words From "The Drone"

Well, thank goodness *that's* over. I don't mind telling you this
has been an extremely difficult translation, not helped at all by
Sma's intransigent and at times obstructive attitude. She frequently used Marain expressions it would be impossible to ren-
der accurately into English without at least a three-dimensional
diagram, and consistently refused to redraft or revise the text
to facilitate its translation. I have done my best, but I can take
no responsibility for any misunderstanding caused by any part
of this communication.

I suppose I had better note here that the chapter titles (including that for Sma's covering letter, and this) and sub-titles are
my own additions. Sma wrote the above as one continuous
document (can you imagine?), but I thought it better to split
the thing up. The chapter titles and sub-titles are, incidentally,
also all names of General Contact Units produced by the *Infra-
caninophile* manufactury in Yinang Orbital which Sma refers to
(without naming) in Chapter Three.

Another thing; you will notice that Sma has the gall to refer
to me simply as "The Drone" in her letter. I have humoured
her matronizing whim quite long enough, and now wish to
make clear that my name is, in fact, Fohristiwhirl Skaffen-
Amtiskaw Handrahen Dran Easpyou. I am not self-important
and it is irresponsible of Sma to suggest that my duties in
Special Circumstances are some sort of atonement for past
misdeeds. *My* conscience is clear.

Skaffen-Amtiskaw.
(Drone, Offensive)

PS: I have met the *Arbitrary*, and it is a much more pleasant
and engaging machine than Sma would have you believe.

# Scratch

OR: The Present and Future of Species HS (sic) Considered as The Contents of a Contemporary Popular Record (qv). Report Abstract/Extract Version 4.2 Begins (after this break);

No one likes to think about what No one likes to think No one likes to think about what might happen happen in the event of your Large Tax-Free Bonus Tax Free Bonus but have you provided for *your* family should your Tax Free Bonus Home Fire Alarm will protect *your* family Large Tax Free better than almost any competing product product Will not Better than almost any product Can you afford *not* to be without this inexpensive Easy Credit Terms Available Easy Easy Easy Credit Terms Available Will not damage carpets.

*I:* Irreversible Neu(t)ral Damage
Absolutely not it's a good idea I told her I said dear these days you've got to look out for number one; go for it, honey. Don't you take any shit about BMW Three Series with discreet spoilers and those bulky overweight mega-diaries with your whole Yuppie life inside those ribbed covers, choosing your Hyper Hyper jacket to go with the new leatherbound you just got Is that a Diver's Watch, do you dive? No is that a Pilot's Briefcase can you fly? Are you sure this is real Perrier? A degree with cloister cred, designer tampons and open-plan toilets. Don't know *anybody* with AIDS yet. This the powder room? Na it's a good good idea I told her go for it honey; cancel BUPA if you have to—feeling all right are you? Get a smear done first, 'course—and sell the Gas shares; remortgage with my cousin he'll see you right and set it up if you want; show

these fucking Grauniad reading wankers what you think of them; a Unit Trust investing only in South Africa, the nuclear and defence industries and tobacco related products products is a great idea. At least you know where you are lets do lunch and talk about it. By the way, is it true about Naomi and Gerald?

*II:* The Base Of The Iceberg
(smell) The crunched up packets of cheap cigarettes, black stencil writing on yellow covers they call them crush-proof in the U.S. all crushdup. The line of dripping washing nappies, socks, nappies, blouse—needs a couple of buttons—more nappies, trousers—from the Oxfam shop—nappies (Intrusion: The economies of scale: stuff the big pinkwhite Pampers box and the E9000 gigasize economy/Family Family Family box of powder into the GTi Don't forget the Comfort. Now then where were we Oh Yes), nappies (smell), tights, nappies, more tights more nappies drip drip drip onto the sheets of newspaper on the floor (the string runs from broken light fitting to the hook holding the faded notice about fire procedure and no guests after ten You are expected to vacate the room for six hours per day Prams must be taken up to rooms Do NOT leave prams in stair wells No cooking in room This door should be should not be wedged open kept locked at all times the building is occupied. Fire proof). The remains of Wimpy meals and McDonald's Complete Family meals and Kentucky Fried Chicken soup in a Basket and Brightly Coloured Shakes and Wendy meals and French Fries (smell) and more French Fries (smell) and a Doner Kebab (small); junk food funk food junk food      fast food for those who queued seven hours at the DHSS today      spent the
                                                                 time in
the park          second hand pair of
a cup last two hours but a skin forms on the top and they chase you out if they're busy
                         fast food

lunchtime                              if it's
raining's the worst
won't allow prams in anyway                    cold in the rain and
the hood leaks
                   keep the curtains drawn all day
                            fast food
(Iknowbut)
Giro don't come til                              next Tuesday
she's been there three days but they've lost the records sent from
               Glasgow what a state poor cow
                            fast food
said it's a respiratory complaint keep him dry I said that's a
joke
                            fast food
         the park
                 station/
                            DHSS/
                   just walk the streets I suppose
(Intrusion: The dripped-on paper sez: WANT A QUICK
LOAN? (homeowners only))
                            fast fod


(meanwhile christ rushed off our feet so busy oh fuck another three-bottle lunch!...Did I pay that with the company
card? Yeah a Vodaphone on the firm next month Oh dear late
again...Let's share a taxi)
                            [fst fwd]
and the tins of beans the cider bottles cough medicine tampon
packets (plus VAT) baby food jars If you dip the French Fries
(plus VAT) in the baby food it makes it last longer won't stop
crying feel like hitting her sometimes I know, she's sick again
(smell) and
                       I'm late again
(sic)                                          what a state
                   fast forward
                      *   *   *

### *III:* Beat Me Up, Scotty

of course there's the spin-offs; Gemini gave us non-stick frying pans, or was it Chuck Yeager? fst fd Well anyway of course there'll be peaceful applications the solar-powered television on my watch would run off the space-based lasers

### *IV:* Hocus, Pocus, Mucus

...that he did, on or about the date given above, wilfully, and while in full possession of his faculties, walk under a ladder without due care and attention, step on the cracks in the pavement (1,345,964 other offences to be taken into consideration), break a mirror (statutory penalty seven years), fail to finish his meat course at dinner (thus incurring a period of rain on the following day of unspecified duration; see attached forensic meteorological report), spill approximately 211 grains of household sodium chloride (common salt: NaCl) without thereafter propelling said same household sodium chloride over and above left shoulder despite supplies of same being freely available, to the furtherance of the Devil's works, and, farther, did, in the presence of several God-fearing witnesses, good men and true, with malice aforethought open an umbrella within a household, as defined by the Household (Definition) Act of the Year of Our Lord...

### *V:* Now Wash Your Hands

I was proceeding in a Westerly direction along Rhodes Street along with others of my gang when I observed the defendant emerging from the premises now known to me as "Singh Brothers Supermarket Halal Meats and Off License," carrying a cardboard container of household supplies and sporting a dark complexion, whereupon my colleagues and I gave chase. The defendant thereupon dropped the said box of household supplies, what I kicked as I persued him. The defendant was chased into what I now know is Crucial Brew Close, where I and others kicked im in the ghoulies, kidnies and head, causing him injury and distress; following which, we ran away.

And I would like to thank the Rascist Bastards Complaints Review Board for helping to keep this sort of thing on the streets (Intrusion: No one asked them to come here I'd send them all back to where they came from (Bradford). Well, before that (Bradford). Well, originally (Shock Deport Report: Royals Repatriated to Hunland/ Wopland; Entire So-Called "English" Upper Class "Relocated" to France in "1066 Effect": East African camps being prepared for "Stand Off Zanzibar" Final Solution. Message Ends).

*VI:* Formula Writing
Junk DNA Junk AND Junk NAD Junk DAN Junk AND nkJu ADN unkJ DNA unkJ AND unkJ NAD unkJ DAN unkJ ADN nkJu DNA nkJu AND nkJu NAD nkJu ADN kJun DNA kJun AND kJun NAD kJun DAN kJun ADN unJk DNA unJk AND unJk NAD unJk DAN (etc) (tce, cet, tec, cet)

*VII:* Thesis, Antithesis, Dialysis
cancel BUPA if you have to New Cancer Research Grant Safe in our hands New Cancer Research Grant Report concludes Safe in our waldos PRIVATE CANCER TREATMENT: A GROWTH INDUSTRY Concludes the poor and unemployed are more susceptible to a wide range of Spending More Than More Than More Than Spending More Than Ever Before New Cancer Research Grant SPENDING MORE THAN EVER BEFORE research cut slashed in NEW CUTS IN round of spending cuts NEW CUTS IN after wide consultations NEW CUTS IN reduced demand NEW CUTS IN catchment area NEW CUTS IN revised priorities NEW CUTS IN community care NEW CUTS IN susceptible to a wide range of NEW CUTS IN NEW CUTS IN CUTS IN SURGICAL…Research Grant will no longer be referred to as a "lump sum" and this latest mark of kidney machine—the twelve-inch dance re-mix laser guided precision munition version—can scatter hundreds of these tiny kidney-stone size machinettes over an area the

size of a squash courts cricket pitch golf course, breaking up
breaking up an enemy kidney failure while it's still in Warsaw
Pict territory (oops, sic) go for it honey.


*VIII:* What Free World
LOONY LEFT BLACK LESBIANS WITH AIDS BAN
ENGLISH IN NURSERIES
ANOTHER
MAGGIE SLAMS "ENEMY WITHIN"
ANOTHER TRIUMPH
"SORRY KIDS, YOU'RE WHITE"
ANOTHER TRIUMPH FOR
BASTARDS!
ANOTHER TRIUMPH FOR BRITAIN
ANOTHER BLOW FOR LABOUR
UNEMPLOYMENT DOWN AGAIN
ANOTHER TRIUMPH FOR BRITAIN
ANOTHER TRIUMPH
LABOUR PLANS SCROUNGERS' CHARTER
ANOTHER TRIUMPH FOR
35,000 JOBS TO GO IF LABOUR WIN
ANOTHER TRIUMPH FOR
CHEERS, MAGGIE!
ANOTHER TRIUMPH FOR
(RECORD PROFITS)
ANOTHER TRIUMPH FOR
U.S.
          GOTCHA!


*IX:* Rapid Ear Movement
out of ten children below the age of six regularly have night-
mares about nuclear war
I                    sed it provides jobs, dunnit, an he sez "So
did Belsin and Outshwits; them cattle trux didn't drive themselves you no; somebody had ta bild the camps and put up
the electric wire and keep the showers hosed down; tok to me

about hard wurk once you've spent all day supervizing frowing
bodies into furnaces"
Iknow      "Ow, ullo Fritz; wotcher doin theez daze?"
           "Well, Kurt, am on a Reich Retraining Scheme,
ineye?; pulling gold teef outa ded Jooz."
Iknowbut        provides jobz alright
Six million? Don't make me larf that's just one city
Iknowbutwhat gas was quick compared to radiation

                                                     sickness
Iknowbutwhatcan      There was this sick cunt made
lightshades outer ther skin but at Hiroshima they woz just
shadders on the wall
Iknowbutwhatcanyou      makes yer fink, dunnit?
Iknowbutwhatcanyoudo?      course that labour lot would
just let the Rushins march right in and you got ta defend
yourself, intya?

*X:* The History Of The Universe In Three Words (sic)
THE HISTORY OF THE UNIVERSE

CHAPTER ONE

Bang!

CHAPTER TWO

sssss...

CHAPTER THREE

crunch.

THE END

*XI:* The Precise Nature Of The Catastrophe
WELCUM TO THE FEWTCHIR makes yer makes yer
fink makes yer course that labour lot would just makes yer
fink makes yer na it's true I read it in the paper (sic) RED

MENACE makes yer fink SPENDING na don't scratch it it'll never get better (sick) march right in march march march right in makes yer fink course there'll be spin-offs KILL AN ARGIE AND WIN A METRO I sed go for it honey KILL A look after number one and KILL A you got ta defend yourself KILL A KILL A fst fd KILL KILL KILL A COMMIE AND it makes you kicked im in the kidnie machines ATTENTION: you got ta SPENDING MORE defend yourself got ta defend your CHALLENGER BOMBS CHERNOBYL WITH LASER GUIDED AIDS self, SEVENTY-THREE SECONDS OVER CAPE CANAVERAL TWELVE MINUTES OVER TRIPOLI ONE HUNDRED THOUSAND YEARS OVER NORTHERN EUROPE, intya? ATTENTION: oh well scratch another power station scratch another planet fst fd I sed ARMING intya? GROWTH without INDUSTRY without due GROWTH GROWTH GROWTH INDUSTRY without due care and SPENDING MORE THAN you got ta defend SPENDING MORE THAN EVER defend your Tax Free GROWTH INDUSTRY without due care and ATTENTION: ARMING SEQUENCE ta defend yourself, intya? just let them Rushins ATTENTION: ARMING SEQUENCE INITIATED fst fd Course fst fd you got ta defend yourself fst fd NO ONE LIKES TO THINK the curtains closed all day fst ds ATTENTION (homeowners only) NO ONE LIKES you got ta NO ONE LIKES TO (Intrusion:) you got ta ATTENTION: Will not damage carpets ATTENTION: I said ATTENTION: fst fd ATTENTION: fst fd ATTENTION: NO ONE LIKES TO defend your SPENDING MORE THAN EVER BEFORE self, intya? I sed go for it ATTENTION: ATTENTION: ATTENTION: Message Ends defend defend defend yourself, intya? you got ta defend you—ullo, wot's that bright l-? ATTENTION:

[EMP]

(sssss…)


*XII:* The End

THE END

# meet the author

Ray Charles Redman

IAIN BANKS came to widespread and controversial public notice with the publication of his first novel, *The Wasp Factory*, in 1984. *Consider Phlebas*, his first science fiction novel, was published under the name Iain M. Banks in 1987 and began his celebrated ten-book Culture series. He is acclaimed as one of the most powerful, innovative, and exciting writers of his generation.

Find out more about Iain M. Banks and other Orbit authors by registering for the free monthly newsletter at orbitbooks.net.

orbit

Follow us:

f /orbitbooksUS

X /orbitbooks

▶ /orbitbooks

Join our mailing list
to receive alerts on our
latest releases and deals.

**orbitbooks.net**

Enter our monthly
giveaway for the chance
to win some epic prizes.

**orbitloot.com**